3 MINUTE
BEDTIME TALES

3 MINUTE
BEDTIME TALES

Written by Nicola Baxter
Illustrated by Andy Everitt-Stewart

ARMADILLO

1 3 5 7 9 10 8 6 4 2

ISBN 10: 1-84322-520-4
ISBN 13: 978-1-84322-520-1

Published by Armadillo Books, an imprint of
Bookmart Limited, Registered Number 2372865
Trading as Bookmart Limited, Blaby Road,
Wigston, Leicester LE18 4SE, England

Produced for Bookmart Limited by
Nicola Baxter
PO Box 215, Framingham Earl,
Norwich Norfolk NR14 7UR

Designer: Amanda Hawkes
Production designer: Amy Barton

Originally published in 2004 by Bookmart Limited as
3 Minute Animal Stories and *3 Minute Bedtime Stories*

Printed in Thailand

This book belongs to

....

Contents

The Dragon

At school, Josh's teacher read the class a story about a dragon. It was very exciting. Josh couldn't think about anything else all day. That night he even had a dream about a dragon. It was frightening and not frightening at the same time.

The next morning Josh was eating his breakfast in the kitchen when he suddenly grabbed his dad's arm, spilling cereal everywhere.

"Look, Dad!" he cried. "There's a dragon in the garden!"

Dad looked out. He saw a little smoke drifting over the fence. "It's just Jim next door having a bonfire," he said. "Look at the state of my sweater!"

Later, Dad went out to cut the grass. Josh followed him. Suddenly, Josh yelled, "Dad! Look at this!"

Dad dropped grass cuttings all over the lawn. Josh was staring at the path. "Dragon footprints!" he cried.

Dad looked and frowned. "Don't be silly," he said. "That's next-door's cat scratching the path again. Now look at the mess on the lawn!"

Josh wasn't convinced. He was pretty sure he saw dragon scratch marks on the fence (though it *could* have been the cat) and dragon bite marks on the cabbages (though it *could* have been slugs). Dad said that if he heard another word about dragons, he might go mad.

Josh went inside. *Thud! Thud!* Could it be a you-know-what?

No, it was just his mother moving the furniture. Josh laughed. He decided to stop thinking about dragons and play in his room instead. He was in for a surprise....

11

The New Village

Once upon a time there was a friendly giant. He lived in a huge castle on a hill. At the bottom of the hill there was a village. The people in the village were the same size as you and me, but they got on pretty well with the giant. He was always careful to keep to the path up the hillside so that his big boots didn't trample the fields around the village.

One day, the giant went to visit a friend. When he was ready to come home, it was already dark.

"I'll lend you a lantern," said his friend.

So the giant set out with his lantern. The moon was shining. It was easy to see the way. But as the giant walked, a storm blew up. Clouds covered the moon. The wind and rain put out the lantern. Suddenly it was wet and cold and very, very dark.

The giant hurried to get home to his warm castle, but he really couldn't see where he was going. *Crunch!* He put his big foot on something in the dark. *Crunch! Crunch!* At last, the giant reached his home and his giant-sized bed.

In the morning, he woke to hear a faint wailing sound. At the bottom of the hill, the people who were the same size as you and me were in a terrible state.

"In the night," they told the giant, "the storm flattened most of the village. Luckily, no one was hurt, as we were at a party further down the valley. But look at our homes! Winter is coming, and we have nowhere to live."

The giant looked at the flattened village. He didn't think the storm had done this. He felt dreadful.

"Let me help," he said. But his huge fingers were too clumsy to build little houses. He just got in the way. What could he do?

Then the giant had a good idea. "My castle is very big," he said. "There would be room for all of you while you rebuild your village."

But that is not quite what happened. The villagers *did* go to stay with the giant, but they were so warm and comfortable in the castle that they never did rebuild their village! And the villagers and the giant lived happily together ever after.

The Magic Potato

Once upon a time there was a lazy little elf. His mother did everything for him. She cooked him three big meals every day (and one or two snacks in between). You will not be surprised to know that he was also quite a plump little elf!

One day, the elf's mother had to go to visit her sister, who was ill. "You'll be fine," she told her son. "I know you love potatoes, so I've left you a big bag in the kitchen. All you have to do is to put them in the oven for delicious baked potatoes."

 The elf did as she said. It was quite easy, and for several weeks he ate baked potatoes for nearly every meal. That was a mistake. Soon, there were only a few potatoes left in the bottom of the bag.

The elf went to the market to buy some more. He knew that was what his mother did when things ran out. But the stallkeepers shook their heads. Oh no, there are no potatoes to be had anywhere, they said. The elf was worried. He telephoned his mother.

"Do not eat the last potatoes," she said. "They are magic. Put them in the ground and wait to see what happens."

The elf was very puzzled, but he did what she said. He knew that his mother's father's sister's cousin had been a fairy, so there was a little magic in the family.

The next morning, there were green shoots where he had planted the potatoes. And by lunchtime, there were tiny yellow flowers as well. By the evening, the leaves and flowers had started to die.

The elf phoned his mother again. He was beginning to feel very hungry. "Well done," she replied. "Now dig where the potato plants grew."

The little elf dug and found, to his amazement, dozens and dozens of potatoes. "It's magic!" he told his mother that evening as he sat, happily full, by the phone.

"It is magic," said his mother, "but anyone can do it. It just happens faster with a fairy in the family."

The elf went to bed, and when he woke up, he had a brilliant idea. He grew some more potatoes and took them to the market! Everyone wanted to buy them. By the time his mother came home, the little elf was happier, fitter and richer than he had ever been before. And he wasn't lazy any more. Maybe that was the real magic!

Wizard Muddle

There was once a bad wizard called Billings. He didn't mean to be bad, but his spells always went wrong. When Mrs. Mumble wanted to make her vegetables grow, his spell made her hair grow! Mr. Hoggle wanted a cure for his headache, but Wizard Billings turned him into a frog!

On the whole, people tried not to ask for Wizard Billings's help, but there are some things you really do need a wizard for. When little Bubble's kitten went missing and couldn't be found, his granny took the little boy to the wizard. There was nothing left to try.

Wizard Billings listened to Bubble's troubles and promised that he could help. "Now where did I put that potion?" he muttered.

Bubble's granny looked around the wizard's cave. It was in a terrible mess. There were bottles and jars everywhere.

Wizard Billings peered at some pink liquid in a tall, thin bottle. "Ah, this is the one," he said.

Granny stopped him just in time.
"This bottle has a label that says,
'Potion for turning things purple!'" she said.
"That's not what we need! Can't you see?"

Wizard Billings shifted uncomfortably, and Granny suddenly understood a great deal.

"Wizard Billings, come with me!" she cried.

She led the wizard and Bubble down the hillside to the office of Miss Blink, the optician.

When Wizard Billings came out half an hour later, he was wearing a smart pair of glasses and grinning broadly.

"I didn't realize I needed glasses," he said.
"How much clearer everything is now. In fact, what is that small, furry thing at the top of that tree?"

"My kitten!" cried Bubble. "Oh no, he's stuck!"

"No problem," cried the wizard. He hurried back to his cave and found a green potion that would do the trick. (On the label, it said, "Mixture for bringing kittens down from trees. Do not use on cows.")

Things are much happier in Wizard Billings's village now. Bubble has his kitten back, the vegetables are huge, and Mr. Hoggle is no longer a frog. Just in case, Wizard Billings has made up a big bottle of potion with a label in huge letters. It says:

Potion for
finding
lost glasses

The Dancing Elephant

Cheeky Monkey swung through the jungle. He spotted his friend Enormous Elephant. "See you tomorrow, Enormous!" shouted Cheeky as he passed.

"Tomorrow?" trumpeted the elephant. "Why, what's happening tomorrow?"

"It's Stripy Tiger's birthday party, of course!" yelled Cheeky, and he disappeared into the trees.

Enormous Elephant was stunned. He hadn't been invited to Stripy's party. Elephants never forget, so he was very sure. But Stripy was one of the elephant's oldest friends. How could he have been left out?

Enormous went home and didn't feel like eating his supper. His mother was worried. Enormous was always hungry! In the end, the elephant told her what had happened.

"That's very strange," said his mother. "I think it must be a mistake. I'll have a little word with Mrs. Tiger."

While Enormous slept, Mrs. Elephant did just what she had promised. She was surprised by the answer.

"That's right," said Mrs. Tiger. "We didn't invite Enormous."

"But why? He's so upset!" cried Mrs. Elephant.

"Oh dear. You see, there are a lot of little ones coming," explained her friend, "and it's a *dancing* party!"

Now Mrs. Elephant understood. When Enormous danced, the whole jungle shook, and certainly it was dangerous for little animals anywhere near his huge feet. But she did feel sorry for her son. It wasn't his fault his feet were so big.

"I've had an idea," she told Mrs. Tiger.

When Stripy's mother heard the idea, she was delighted.

The next day, Enormous went happily along to the party with all his friends. When the dancing started, some of the animals looked anxiously at Enormous, but the huge animal smiled. "Dancing isn't just about moving your feet," he said. "I can do a kind of dancing that none of you can!"

"What do you mean?" cried his friends.

"I mean *trunk* dancing!" laughed Enormous. And he swayed and wiggled his trunk to the music in the most wonderful way, without ever moving his feet at all.

Everyone agreed it was the best party ever, and Enormous's trunk dancing was fantastic, especially when he lifted up the birthday tiger. Then the party really went with a swing!

Up, Up and Away!

When Farmer Harris heard that a little boy in the village needed money for a special chair to help him get around, he was determined to help. He decided to have an Open Day on his farm.

For weeks, Farmer Harris got ready for the big day. He even polished his tractor and trailer so he could give rides around the farm.

He persuaded his sister to run a cake stall, and made lots of lemonade. He planned a treasure hunt for the older children. But what about the little ones? Farmer Harris got in touch with a shop in town and persuaded them to bring hundreds of helium-filled balloons at a very reasonable price.

When the day arrived, the farmer was amazed by how many people attended. He stood near the gate, holding huge bunches of balloons in each hand, welcoming all who came, young and old.

Farmer Harris was especially pleased when the little boy who needed the chair arrived in his mother's arms.

"Can we have a photo?"
called a newspaper reporter.
"Give him a balloon.
It will look great."

But Farmer Harris was so keen
to be kind that he didn't give
just one balloon. He gave Sean
two whole bunches of balloons!

Sean was a very small boy. As soon
as he grabbed the balloons, he
started to rise up into the air!

"Help!" cried his mother.

"Help!" cried Farmer Harris.

"Wheee!" cried Sean. "This is FUN!"

The grown-ups watched in
amazement as Sean floated off over
the farm. They chased him through the farmyard … and through
the fields (scaring the scarecrow) … and over the hills (surprising
the sheep) … and back down the lane to the barnyard. This time,
some of the balloons caught on the weathervane, leaving Sean
sitting on top of the roof!

Farmer Harris rushed out with his long ladder and soon
rescued the little boy. He carried him over to his family.

"I'm so, so sorry…," he began.

But Sean's mother smiled. "Look at his face," she said.
"He's had a wonderful adventure. Let's not say another word."

But there *was* another word to say to Farmer Harris; "Thanks!" The
picture of Sean flying appeared in every newspaper in the country, and
enough money arrived to buy chairs for hundreds of children like him.

The Christmas Tree

Christy lived in a big house. There was a hallway with a huge staircase winding up from it. At Christmas, Christy's dad brought in an enormous Christmas tree that stretched nearly to the ceiling far above. It was decorated with all sorts of shining ornaments and tinsel. It looked wonderful. Christy didn't know anyone who had such a big and beautiful tree.

One year, Christy's dad told her that the whole family was going to move for a while. He had a job at a college far away. It wasn't for ever, but it was too far to travel backwards and forwards.

"We'll live in a little flat for a year," said Dad. "It will be fun."

And it was fun, until it came to Christmas. One morning, Christy came down to breakfast to find a tiny little tree sitting on a small table.

"We haven't got room for a big tree," said her mother, "but this little one is fun, isn't it?"

Christy looked at the tiny tree in disgust. "That's not a tree," she said. "It's just silly. I want a big tree like the one we had last year."

Outside the window, there was a huge pine tree. "That's the kind of tree we want," said Christy, pointing.

"It wouldn't fit in here!" laughed her mother. "It wouldn't even come through the door. And anyway, we haven't got any of our decorations or lights here."

But she found it hard to forget Christy's disappointed face, and on Christmas Eve, she had an idea. Christy's dad borrowed a ladder and tied all sorts of things to the tree outside. There were seeds and nuts and bright red apples. There were garlands of peanuts in their shells threaded together and upsidedown coconut shells. It looked rather strange.

"Do you think this will work?" asked Dad.

"Wait and see," smiled Christy's mother.

On Christmas Day, when Christy looked out of the window, the tree was filled with birds and squirrels, all happily pecking and nibbling away.

"It's even better than our tree back at home!" cried Christy.

So always after that, Christy's family had two Christmas trees, an indoor one and an outdoor one. You might like to try it, too.

One Fish, Two Fish

There was once a little orange fish who lived in the warm blue waters of the Indian Ocean. One day he was playing hide-and-seek with his mother in and out of the coral.

"Count to ten," said his mother, "then come and find me."

So the little fish counted out loud. "One, two, three, six, eight, ten! I'm coming!"

"Hey," said the mother fish, "that's not right! Start again!"

So the little fish put his fins over his eyes and began, "One, two, three, four, nine, seven, ten! Coming!"

When he looked up, his mother was not hiding. "Little fish," she said firmly, "we need to do some work on your counting. That wasn't right at all. Look, there are lots of friends to count right here."

"One crawly crab!" cried the little fish. "Two yellow fish! Now what?"

"Three of us!" cried his mother. "You, me and Dad, who is snoozing behind that rock. Look!"

"Three orange fish!" cried the little one. "Er…."

"It's simple," said his mother. "Four little starfish, five wiggly eels, six striped swimming fish, seven purple puffer fish, eight legs on Oscar octopus, nine speedy red fish, and ten tiny turtles. Now you try."

The little fish counted, "One crawly crab, two yellow fish, three orange fish, four little starfish … oh no! The wiggly eels are wiggling! I can't count them when they're moving. And the six striped swimming fish are worse!"

The little fish's mother saw that it was true. "Just a minute," she said.

The next moment, the little fish heard, "Smile, please!" and not long after, his proud parents brought him a beautiful big photograph of the undersea world. He could easily count now that everyone was still. Can you help him?

The Hungry Bear

There was once a bear who lived in a cave in a forest. He was a very nice bear and never troubled anyone except once a year in the springtime. You see, that was when he woke up from his winter's sleep, and when he woke up he was very, very hungry. That made everyone else very, very worried.

One year, on the first fine day of spring, the bear woke up and stretched. He had only one thing on his mind: food! He stomped off down the forest path.

The first creature he met was a squirrel.

"I'm going to eat you!" said the bear. And he did! But he was in such a hurry that he swallowed the squirrel whole, and he could feel the little animal scampering up and down inside him as he walked along.

Next he came to a lane, where a cat was chasing a mouse. In one gulp, the bear ate the cat and the mouse! But the cat was still chasing the mouse inside the bear. It felt very funny.

The bear was still hungry, and when he saw a field of sheep, he jumped over the fence and swallowed the nearest one. But the sheep was a ram. With his big horns he kept butting the bear from inside! Ouch!

By the time a little boy came walking down the lane, the bear was feeling rather poorly and sitting down.

The boy was not frightened. He put his hands on his hips and said firmly, "It's your own fault, you know. Come with me. I think I can help."

The boy ran off, leaving the bear to trot after him. It was not very comfortable, and as the bear jogged up and down, the big ram jumped right out of his mouth. That felt much better. Then, as the bear followed the boy over a fence, the cat and the mouse jumped out. Aaah! That was better still.

Last of all, as the boy and the bear came tumbling down a hill, the squirrel jumped out. Phew! The bear felt fine except … he was very hungry again!

The boy threw open the doors of a big barn. Inside, the villagers had filled a table with pies and cakes! With a growl of delight, the bear rushed in and began to eat.

"Each year," said the boy, "we'll make you lots of good things to eat at the beginning of spring, if you promise not to eat our cats or dogs or sheep or cows! Is it a deal?"

The bear couldn't say a word. His mouth was too full of pies and cakes. But, picking up another pie, he nodded his head. He has never been a problem since.

Patty Pig

Patty Pig was the youngest of eight brothers and sisters. They were all pink, cheeky pigs with curly tails. It was very hard to tell them apart, but Mamma Pig and Papa Pig always seemed to manage it.

Still Patty Pig wasn't happy. "I want to be different," she muttered to herself.

One day, Patty Pig was munching some carrots in the barnyard when she saw something interesting. It was a huge, muddy puddle!

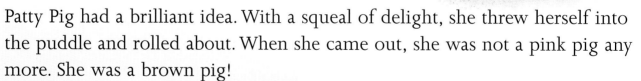

Patty Pig had a brilliant idea. With a squeal of delight, she threw herself into the puddle and rolled about. When she came out, she was not a pink pig any more. She was a brown pig!

"Hah!" said Patty Pig. "Now I'm different!"

But behind her she suddenly heard a lot more squeals of delight. Her brothers and sisters, seeing their muddy sister, thought rolling in the puddle was a great idea. In seconds, there were eight brown piglets in the yard.

Patty Pig frowned. Then she grinned.
She rushed over to the duckpond and
threw herself in with a massive SPLASH!

When she came out, all the mud was gone.
"Hah! I'm the only pink piglet," she giggled.

You can guess what happened next.
With deafening squeals and splashes
and sploshes everywhere, the seven
muddy piglets also jumped into the pond.
Soon, eight pink piglets were back in the yard.

Patty Pig was upset. Mamma Pig and Papa Pig noticed
and asked her what was the matter. Poor Patty explained.

Then Mamma and
Papa laughed out
loud. "But Patty,"
they cried, "you *are*
different. You don't
need to worry
about that at all!"

"How?" sniffed
Patty Pig.

"You are different
because, although
you were born last,
you are *always* the
first to do anything
new. You are a *very*
special piglet."

You are very special, too! Why don't you ask the grown-up
who is sharing this book with you just how special you are?

The Mouse in the Clock

There was once a mouse who lived in a grandfather clock. The clock stood in a corner of the hall of a very old house. It hadn't worked for years. Inside the clock, the little mouse had plenty of room to run about and a snug little space at the top, behind the face, where she slept. She was very happy in her home.

One day the old man who lived in the house had a visit from his sister. She was a bossy woman.

"Alfred! You should have that clock mended," she said.

The old man knew that she would go on and on and on until she got her way, so the next day he called a clock-mender.

The man who came to look at the clock smiled. "This is a fine old clock," he said, "and there probably isn't much wrong with it. I might be able to have it working for you by lunchtime."

He opened the case, and the little mouse scurried out of a hole at the back and hid under the stairs.

It didn't take the man long to get the clock working.

"I think you've had mice in here," he told the old man. "You'll need to watch that."

Well before lunchtime, the clock-mender was gone, and the little mouse crept back into her home. It felt very different. For a start, there was the loud ticking. *Tick, tick, tick, tick....* It went on and on. Then there was a big metal thing swinging dangerously backwards and forwards in the case. It was the pendulum, but the little mouse didn't know that.

Worse was to come. At a quarter past eleven, the clock struck. *Ding, dong, ding, dong, ding, dong, ding, dong!* At half past, it chimed the same tune twice. At a quarter to the hour, the chimes happened three times! But at twelve o'clock there was a dreadful noise. *DONG! DONG! DONG! DONG! DONG! DONG! DONG! DONG! DONG! DONG! DONG! DONG!*

The little mouse was so unhappy. How could she live like this? Forgetting to hide, she sat outside the clock with her paws over her ears. Suddenly, she realized the old man was standing next to her.

"It's awful," he said. "I've loved the peace of this house for seventy years, and now it's ruined. I can't stand it!"

He looked down and noticed the little mouse. A look of understanding came over his face. "This can be our secret," he whispered. And he carefully opened the clock's case, took out the long metal pendulum, and walked quietly away with it.

That night, everyone in the huge old house was happy again.

The Magic Eggs

There was once a farmer who had a fat, brown hen called Mildred. She laid beautiful white eggs, which the farmer enjoyed every day for his breakfast.

One morning, when he went to see Mildred for his breakfast egg, the farmer had a big surprise.

"Certainly not!" said the hen (who usually only said, "Cluck!") She gave the farmer a sharp peck on the hand and put her beak in the air.

"What's going on here?" said the farmer crossly. "I won't have a hen telling me what to do! Give me that egg!"

"No!" said the hen. "This is a magic egg. I can't give it to you."

The farmer decided not to risk another peck. He went back into the farmhouse and thought about what Mildred had said. A magic egg? There were no such things! On the other hand, he hadn't thought there were talking hens, either.

All that day, the farmer thought and thought. He remembered all the stories he had ever heard about magic when he was a boy. He couldn't think of any where magic was a *bad* thing. Perhaps the egg would give him three wishes!

The next day, Mildred again refused to let the farmer take an egg. "This one is magic, too," she said. Now she was sitting on two of them.

Two magic eggs! Could that mean (the farmer had to count on his fingers) *six* wishes?

The next day, and the next day, and the day after that, the same thing happened. Soon Mildred was sitting on six magic eggs, and the farmer had done lots of sums on bits of paper and worked out that he had eighteen wishes to come.

"I'm going to be rich!" he crowed. "I'm going to have a beautiful wife, and three fine sons, and three lovely daughters. I'm going to have a huge farm, and a fine horse to take me to church on Sundays. I'm going to have new suits of clothes and the best boots in the country. A famous artist will paint my portrait. I'll have dancing lessons. I'll … I'll …." But the farmer couldn't think of any more wishes, though he still had eight left.

Three weeks later, the farmer had a shock. Each one of Mildred's eggs hatched … and out hopped eight fluffy chicks!

The farmer was furious, but Mildred smiled. She thought those eggs had been pretty magical after all. What do you think?

The Scarecrow

Rufus was excited. His village was holding a scarecrow competition. The idea was that each family would make a scarecrow and put it up in the front garden. The judges would walk through the village and choose a winner.

Rufus's dad grew vegetables for a living, so he knew a lot about scarecrows. Rufus was sure he would win. He found two stout branches in the hedgerow and tied them into a cross-shape with some string. Then he pushed the longest branch into the ground and fixed a big turnip on the top to make a head.

Rufus felt he had made a great start. Now all he had to do was to find some clothes for his scarecrow. That should be easy.

It wasn't. "Can I have your old hat for my scarecrow?" Rufus asked his dad.

"Certainly not," said Dad. "I'm still wearing it."

"What about your old jacket?"

"What, my nearly-new jacket with the small tear in the sleeve?" Dad replied. "You must be joking!"

It was the same when Rufus asked about trousers,
a scarf, and an old pair of wellies.

"I need those wellies," said Dad firmly,
"even though I don't wear them any more.
You never know when they might come in handy."

Rufus was desperate. He even tried to find some old clothes of
his own to use, but they were much too small. Grandad was no
good either. He wanted to hang on to his old suits and shoes.

"Now you know where your dad gets it from!"
grinned Rufus's mother. "Let me have a think."

When she spoke to him the next day, Rufus
wanted to cry. "That's not right at all,"
he said. "Everyone will laugh!"

But he didn't have any choice, so Rufus
dressed his scarecrow in a pair of tights
stuffed with straw, a pair of green
shoes, an orange and pink skirt, a
yellow and blue jumper (also stuffed
with straw), a red, curly wig, and a
huge, flowery hat that his mother
had once worn to a wedding. His
was the only female scarecrow,
and he thought it looked *awful*.

But later that week, the judges came
around. "A clear winner!" laughed
one of them. "I'm sure this
lady's dreadful fashion sense
would frighten any crow!"

"Well, really!" said Rufus's mother.
But she said it very quietly indeed.

The Crown Crisis

There was once a princess who loved to play outside with all her bird and animal friends. She liked this much better than pretty clothes and jewels.

One day, when she was having a wonderful game chasing some baby bunnies through the forest, her golden crown got caught on a tree. The princess didn't even notice it was missing until she sat down to rest an hour later.

"Oh no!" she cried. "What will the king and queen say! I must find it!" But although she looked hard, she couldn't remember at all where she had been. The forest was very large, and the crown wasn't.

At last, the princess started to cry. "Don't worry," said a little bird. "I can build beautiful nests from twigs and leaves. I'll make you a new crown."

The little bird worked hard, and the crown fitted beautifully. But when the princess looked at herself in a forest pool, she started to cry again. "It's all stiff and brown," she sobbed. "I look as if I've got a bird's nest on my head!"

"Don't worry," croaked a green frog in the pool.
"I can make something that will glisten and glitter,
just like your real crown. Wait just a minute."
He dived down to the bottom of the
pool and came up with a shining,
glittering crown! Water droplets
shone on it like diamonds but …
it was made of slimy pondweed!
The princess shuddered and
began to cry again.

Now all this time, one bright-eyed bird had kept quiet.
He knew exactly where the princess's real crown was,
for his sharp eyes had spotted its
sparkle among the leaves.

The magpie loved anything shiny or
glittering. He had planned to get
the crown later and keep it for
himself. Even *his* greedy heart was
touched, however, by the princess's
tears. Without a word, he flew off to
get the crown.

When the princess saw the crown in
the magpie's beak, she almost started
crying again … with joy this time!
Instead, she thanked the magpie and
promised that she would never forget
him, which is why, on her coat of
arms, a cheeky black and white bird
has pride of place!

The Kite Tangle

When Grandad came to visit, he always brought presents for Hattie, Jack, Kizzy and Shane. That should have been a good thing, but instead it usually led to arguments. Hattie said Jack's present was bigger. Shane wanted the book that Kizzy had been given. Grandad got fed up. "Next time I come," he said, "I'm going to bring you all exactly the same present. Then there'll be no quarrelling."

And that's just what he did … well, nearly. Grandad brought each of the four children a beautiful, bright kite! Each was exactly the same except for one thing. One was red. One was blue. One was green and one was yellow.

You can guess what happened.

"I'll have the red one!" cried Kizzy.

"No! I want the red one!" Jack yelled.

"That's not fair! I want it!" said Shane.

"I've already got my hand on it," said Jack.

Grandad looked grim. "This is hopeless," he said. "Put on your hats and coats, all of you, and your gloves, too. It's a lovely windy day but it's very cold. I'll decide who is having what as we walk up the hill."

On top of the hill, the children were soon having a wonderful time flying their kites, and there were no arguments at all! Clever Grandad! Can you follow the strings to work out how he decided who had which kite?

Where's That Book?

Professor Puffle was the wisest elf in Elfland. He knew almost everything there was to know, and if there was something he wasn't sure about, he looked it up in one of his books.

Professor Puffle had rooms and rooms full of books. Luckily, he was a very tidy elf, and he had a special book called a catalogue. It listed all the books in his library and told him just where to find them.

But the time came when the professor's little toadstool house simply wasn't big enough for all his books. He would have to move. Luckily, he soon found just the thing. It was a hollow tree-trunk. There was plenty of space in the tall trunk for hundreds of bookshelves.

"But how will I reach them?" wondered Professor Puffle.

Bangle Elf, the carpenter, had the answer. "When I build your bookshelves, I will also make you a basket on a rope," she said. "You will be able to pull yourself up and down and lean across to reach any book you like."

It sounded like an excellent plan. The very next day, while Professor Puffle was out visiting friends, she and her helpers were very busy indeed.

When the professor came home that afternoon, all the shelves were finished, and there were books stretching up towards the ceiling far, far above.

"It's wonderful," said the professor faintly. "But … er … did you put my books in order?"

There was a silence. The books were all muddled up!

"Don't worry, my friends," said the professor at last. "It was kind of you to help. I'll sort all the books out. First, I need to find my catalogue. It is blue with orange stripes."

Can you help to find the professor's special book, so that he can start to sort out his library?

Polly's Party

Polly was very excited. It was her friend Amy's birthday. She was having a big party, and Polly wanted to be the prettiest girl there.

After lunch, Polly disappeared into her bedroom.

"It's a bit early to start getting ready, Polly!" called her mother, but Polly didn't listen. She knew it might take a long time to decide what to wear.

Polly was lucky. She had lots of pretty clothes. First she tried on her blue dress with ribbons. It looked lovely. But what if there was lots of dancing? The ribbons might get in the way.

Polly tried on her purple velvet trousers and a sparkly pink top. Just right for dancing. But what if all the other girls were wearing dresses?

Polly put on a short, flowery skirt and a top with frills around the sleeves. That was good, too, but was it quite smart enough for a party?

Polly had an idea. In a box on top of her cupboard was the bridesmaid's dress she had worn when her aunty got married the year before. It was absolutely beautiful, in blue satin, with little pearl flowers on the top part.

Polly carefully pulled the dress out of the box and over her head. Oh dear! The party girl had grown in the last year, but the dress hadn't. It was much too tight to wear.

After that, Polly tried on three more dresses. None of them was right. When her mother came up to see how she was getting on, she found Polly sitting in the middle of a huge pile of clothes, crying.

"Whatever is the matter?" she asked. "And what is all this mess?"

Polly told her. "I haven't got anything to wear!" she sobbed. "At least, not the right thing!"

Polly's mother hid a smile. "Polly, you are silly," she said. "You don't have to wear any of these clothes. Don't you remember? It's a fancy dress party! You can wear your fairy princess outfit!"

Polly looked lovely in her princess costume. But then I think she looked lovely in everything, don't you?

The Magic Flower

Once upon a time there was a very naughty little elf called Billo. He was much too little to learn how to do magic, but he wanted to try.

"How do you make magic fairy dust?" he asked Fairy Mary one day.

"That's a secret," said Fairy Mary. "It comes from a very special flower, deep in the Enchanted Wood. There is only one flower in the world that gives my kind of fairy dust, and only I know which one it is. Even when you find the flower, you can only shake out the dust if you have a silken purse to put it in."

Little Billo thought about this. He knew that fairy dust would help him to do all sorts of magic. The naughty elf decided to follow Fairy Mary next time she went into the Enchanted Wood to find the special flower.

Early one morning, Fairy Mary set out, carrying her silken purse. Billo tiptoed after her. It was fairly easy to follow her secretly through the wood because he could always hide behind a tree if she turned around.

After a long walk, Fairy Mary came to a big meadow. It was full of flowers. Fairy Mary walked right into the middle of it and shook a little blue flower into her purse. Then she hurried home.

Meanwhile, Billo had seen which flower she had shaken, and he didn't take his eyes off it. As soon as the fairy had gone, he hurried straight to it. But in his excitement, Billo had forgotten to bring a silk purse! He ran home to get one, but before he went, he popped his blue cap over the flower so he would know which one it was when he returned.

Billo got back to the meadow in record time, but he had a big surprise. Fairy Mary had done some clever magic of her own. Billo didn't find the fairy dust after all, which is probably just as well.

The Flying Rabbit

Bettina Bunny wanted to fly. I don't mean that she wanted to go in an aeroplane. I mean that she wanted to be able to flap her wings and soar into the air, just like the birds she watched from the roots of the old oak tree where she lived with her family.

There was only one problem. Bettina didn't *have* any wings.

"That's perfectly normal for a rabbit," said her father, when she complained. "You have four furry paws and two enormous ears. That should be enough for any bunny."

That gave Bettina an idea. Her ears really *were* enormous. They were just as big as some birds' wings. Surely she could fly with those?

Bettina went up to the top of a nearby hill and started flapping her ears. It was hard work. She tried hopping up and down as she did it. No good. Then she tried running down the hill while she flapped her ears. She fell over her feet before she got halfway down, and ended up rolling all the way to her home in the tree roots.

"Whatever are you doing, Bettina?" asked her mother, when she had picked herself up. "And why are your ears so droopy?"

"They're tired," said Bettina. And she explained what she had been doing.

Bettina's mother took her daughter outside and sat down with her.

"Now, Bettina," she said, "look at those cows over there. Can they fly?"

"No," said Bettina.

"That's because no one is good at everything, but everyone is good at something. Cows are good at giving milk and mooing. Birds are good at flying and singing. What are bunnies good at?"

"Jumping," said Bettina, looking a little happier.

"And cuddles," said her mother, putting her paws around her daughter.

Bettina liked jumping. She was glad she wasn't a bird after all. She didn't think they were very cuddly at all. She hugged her mother back and jumped away to play. Her ears looked happier, too!

Rowan's Pet

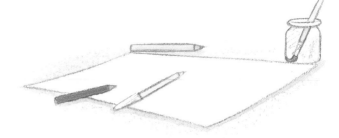

Rowan really wanted a pet, but he lived at the top of a tall building. His mother said there were rules about not being able to keep animals there. It didn't stop Rowan really wishing he could have one.

Things got worse when Rowan's preschool decided to have a fundraising day in the park. One of the events was to be a Grand Pet Show. All the children were really excited about bringing their pets. There were going to be prizes for the biggest pet, the fluffiest pet, the most unusual pet, the friendliest pet, and so on.

Rowan was determined not to be left out. On the day of the Pet Show, he marched into the tent where it was being held with a big sheet of paper rolled up.

The judges moved down the tables, making notes about each of the pets. There were fluffy rabbits, squiggly lizards, sleepy hamsters and chirping birds. One little girl had even brought worms in a kind of glass box filled with soil.

When they reached Rowan, the judges looked up kindly. "Can you show us your pet?" they asked.

"I can!" said Rowan proudly, and he unrolled a beautiful picture of a huge, floppy-eared rabbit with a pink nose. "His name is William," said Rowan.

"Well, that's a beautiful picture," said one of the judges, "but where is your rabbit?"

Rowan smiled. "In here," he said proudly, and he pointed to his head.

The judges looked at each other. "So he's an imaginary rabbit?" they asked. "He isn't a real rabbit?"

"He's very real to me," said Rowan firmly. "And what's more, he can do tricks. He can turn somersaults and jump high buildings. Sometimes he can do some magic, too."

"That's amazing," said the judges.

At the end of the Pet Show, it seemed as if every pet received a prize. The Smallest Mouse, the Wiggliest Worm, the Cheekiest Kitten all had ribbons. At last, only Rowan was left. "Honey, only real live pets can win prizes," whispered his mother. But she was wrong.

"And now we come to our final and most important prize," said the chief judge. "To Rowan goes the top prize for Most Extraordinary Pet." And everybody cheered.

Tomorrow, Tomorrow

Jackson knew that his birthday wasn't very far away. He couldn't wait. "Is it tomorrow, Mum?" he asked.

"No, honey," said his mother. "It's at the end of next week."

"You mean tomorrow, tomorrow, Mum?" Jackson was only a little boy. It was his way of describing the day after tomorrow.

Mum held up eight fingers in front of Jackson and counted them slowly. "It's in one day, two days, three days, four days, five days, six days, seven days, eight days!" she smiled.

"Oh," said Jackson, "you mean tomorrow, tomorrow, tomorrow, tomorrow, tomorrow, tomorrow, tomorrow, tomorrow!"

Mum counted on her fingers again. "Well, yes, that's right," she said, "but Jackson, that's not how we say it."

Jackson didn't hear. He had run off to tell his toys. Now he had the tomorrows straight in his head, he didn't need to listen any more.

The next day, when he bounced on Mum's tummy bright and early in the morning, Jackson said, "Guess what, Mum? My birthday's tomorrow, tomorrow, tomorrow, tomorrow, tomorrow, tomorrow, tomorrow!"

Sleepily, his mother worked it out. "That's right, Jackson," she yawned.

It was the same every morning. Jackson's mother awoke to a string of tomorrows, and Jackson grew more excited each day.

When there were four tomorrows left, Mum couldn't stand it any more. She bought a calendar for Jackson and put it up near his bed. She showed him how to cross off each day when it began, and she drew a big present on the day that was his birthday. For three days, she had peace in the mornings. Jackson could see his birthday was getting closer. He didn't need to keep reciting tomorrows.

The next day, the birthday came at last. Mum heard Jackson thudding down the landing on his way to jump on her in the morning.

"No more tomorrows, Jackson!" she laughed, as her son hurtled in.

"No!" yelled Jackson, as he landed *oomph* on her tummy as usual. "It's today, today, today, today, today, today, today, today, today, today, today, today…!"

The Big Little Brother

When Sarah told her friends she was going to have a little brother, they were very excited.

"I love babies," said Mia. "He'll have little tiny fingers and little tiny toes. Lovely!"

"Well…," began Sarah, but Gina rushed in.

"We could make a mobile to put over his cot," she said. "We could paint pretty fish … or little boats … or stars and a moon! I love making mobiles."

"I know, but…," said Sarah. Emma was bouncing up and down with excitement.

"We've got lots of toys from when my brother was born," she said. "He's at school now, so I'm sure you could have some of them for your baby. When is he going to be born?"

"Actually, I think…," Sarah started to speak, but Gina, looking wise and grown up broke in.

"Oh, I know about that," she said. "It won't be for a few months yet. Your mum doesn't look fat at all. After the holidays, I should think."

"Yes, that's right," said Sarah, "but…."

"Maybe he'll be born in September, like me!" cried Mia.

"Yes, his birthday will be September the fifth," Sarah yelled, "And his name will be Ben. But listen…."

It was no good. All the girls started chattering excitedly. They were very impressed that Sarah knew *exactly* when her brother's birthday would be.

The rest of the school year passed. It was holiday time. On the first day back at school after the holidays, Sarah came into the playground with a big grin on her face.

"He's here," she said. She was holding hands with a little boy of three with blonde hair and a shy smile. "This is Ben."

"But…," said Gina.

"But…," said Mia.

"But, I thought…," said Emma.

"You didn't let me tell you Ben was going to be my adopted brother," said Sarah. "And by the way, he really *loves* mobiles."

The Forgetful Fairy

"Fairy Fennel! Fairy Fennel!" called Mrs. Iggle. "I need your help right away!" She hammered on the door of Fairy Fennel's toadstool cottage.

Fairy Fennel opened her door with a worried look, but Mrs. Iggle didn't notice. "It's my Bert's back," she said. "He can't move a muscle. He's bent over like an ironing board, and he can't straighten up. We need you to come at once."

"Well…," began Fairy Fennel, but Mrs. Iggle wouldn't stop.

"He can't go on like this. How's he going to fit into bed? Come on, there's no time to lose!"

"But…," Fairy Fennel tried again.

"No buts," said Mrs. Iggle impatiently. "Put on your fairy cloak and come! Have a thought for my Bert!"

"You see…," Fairy Fennel tried to explain.

"I do see. I see a man in his prime bent double like an old fellow three times his age," protested her visitor. "I see someone who can't get his own shirt off. I see moaning and groaning all night that will keep me awake. For pity's sake, Fairy Fennel, pick up your wand and come!"

"That's just it," said Fairy Fennel, speaking very, very quickly. "Wand. Lost. Help? No. Sorry!"

"WHAT? Slow down!" cried Mrs. Iggle. At last the story came out. Fairy Fennel had lost her wand. She couldn't help anyone until she found it.

"You leave this to me," said Mrs. Iggle. "I'll go and get Bert to help look. We're good at finding things. I'll be back in a minute."

Sure enough, in a minute, Mrs. Iggle was back with Bert. She searched high up in Fairy Fennel's house, and Bert searched low down, for obvious reasons. Which of them do you think found the wand? Can you see it?

The Best Planet

One night, Annie Jones woke up to find a little green and pink person standing in the middle of her room. It (you really couldn't tell if it was a he or a she) seemed to glow, but not in a scary way. "Who are you?" gasped Annie.

"I'm Tig," said the person. "I come from a planet far, far, far, far, far…."

"Yes, yes, I see," Annie interrupted. "It's a long way away. What's your planet called?"

"Ig," said Tig.

Annie looked at her alien visitor with interest. "Have you visited any other planets?" she asked. "Earth is a bit boring. I was wondering if there was somewhere else I could live."

"Boring how?" said the alien.

"Horrible food at school," said Annie, "and a little brother who steals my crayons. Oh, and not being allowed to stay up and watch *Beryl, Magic Princess* because it's on too late. And helping tidy up on Saturdays."

"On Neopolita," said Tig, "there are four thousand different kinds of ice cream."

"That sounds good," grinned Annie. "I love ice cream after sausage and chips."

"Oh, there aren't any sausages and chips," said Tig. "Only ice cream. Maybe you'd prefer Merevil, where there are no little brothers."

"Magic!" cried Annie. "Can I have a little sister instead?"

"No, no. There are no little children at all. You would be the youngest by about sixty years," Tig explained. "On Palacia, where everyone is a magic princess, you would be, too. They have beautiful dresses and gorgeous hairstyles, and the prettiest shoes you've ever seen."

"Perfect!" cried Annie. "How do I get there? I can't wait to do magic and fight evil trolls and ride unicorns."

"Er, you won't be able to do that, I'm afraid," said Tig. "The princesses are only allowed to sit down all day, in case they mess up their dresses or their hair or their shoes."

Annie frowned. "I expect there is a planet where I wouldn't have to help my mother tidy up," she said.

"Oh yes," replied Tig. "On Varia, there are no mothers at all. Everyone there is a little sad, but you can't have everything."

The next morning, Annie jumped up and gave her little brother a hug, before tidying her bedroom. Her mother had to ask her if she was feeling all right.

"I'm just glad to be on this planet," said Annie, which made no sense to anyone else. But you understand, don't you?

The Apple Tree

Bobbie Bunny loved apples, and he was lucky enough to have a huge apple tree in his garden. When the summer sun was still warm, but there was a smell of woodsmoke in the air, the tree was full of apples. Each day they grew rosier and riper.

"Can we pick the apples today?" Bobbie asked his mother.

"Not yet," came the reply. "I'll tell you when."

But Bobbie couldn't wait. He pestered his mother at least ten times a day. "Is it time yet? They look very ripe to me," he said. "Apples can get too ripe, you know."

But the reply was always the same. "Not yet. I'll tell you when."

Bobbie looked up at the tree. Could he perhaps climb up and just, well, test for himself if the apples were ready?

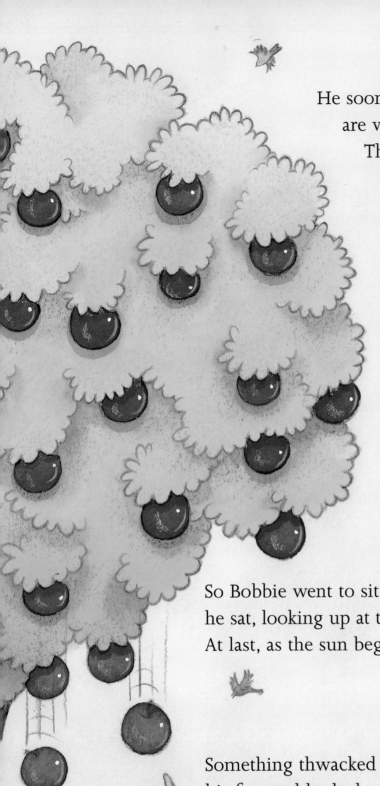

He soon found that he couldn't. Bunnies are very good at hopping and digging. They are very bad at climbing trees. Mrs. Bunny kept the ladder locked up in the shed where little paws couldn't reach it.

In the afternoons, after school, Bobbie could only think of the apples. One day, he told his mother, "I don't care what you say. I'm going to sit under the apple tree until the apples are ripe. Even if it takes days and days and days."

"You'll get pretty cold and hungry," said his mother, "but it's up to you."

So Bobbie went to sit under the apple tree. He sat and he sat, looking up at the apples hanging high above him. At last, as the sun began to sink in the sky, he fell asleep.

Boink!

Something thwacked Bobbie on the nose! He jumped to his feet and looked around. Whatever had happened? His mother, coming out of the house at that moment, laughed.

"Bobbie," she said, "I said I would tell you when, but the tree has done it for me. The apples are ready!"

That night, Bobbie went to bed a very happy bunny. He didn't even think about his sore nose with a tummy full of the sweetest, juiciest apples he had ever tasted.

The Rainbow River

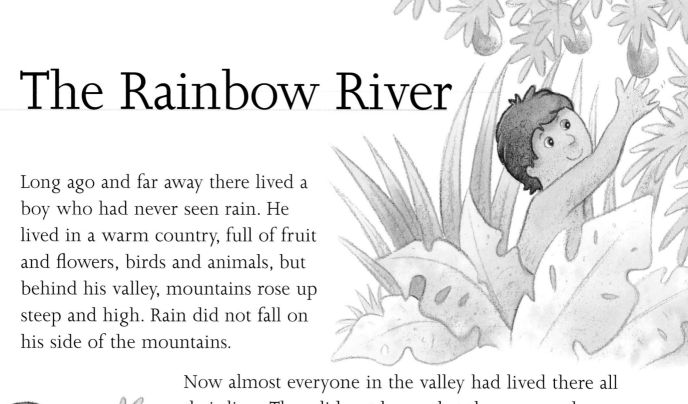

Long ago and far away there lived a boy who had never seen rain. He lived in a warm country, full of fruit and flowers, birds and animals, but behind his valley, mountains rose up steep and high. Rain did not fall on his side of the mountains.

Now almost everyone in the valley had lived there all their lives. They did not know that there were places where there was rain and snow and hard, stinging hail.

It was different for the boy. He had an uncle who had journeyed to many lands. The uncle came back with wonderful stories of storms at sea, and he told the boy about something else, as well. He spoke of a beautiful bow in the sky, called a rainbow, that appeared when the sun shone and the rain came down at the same time.

From the moment he heard about it, the boy could not get rainbows out of his mind. He longed to see one, but he understood that while he stayed in the valley, he never would. And so he made plans to leave as soon as he was old enough.

But when he *was* old enough, the man (for he was no longer a boy) found that he could not go. His parents were old and needed help. Later on, he had a wife and family of his own. At last, he was too old himself to climb the mountains and find a rainbow in the world beyond.

But the river that flowed through the valley was a magic river. It knew the secrets of the old man's heart. On the day that he walked down to the river for the last time, the magic waters prepared a wonderful surprise for him. The river was suddenly full of bright little fish, and the old man was content at last as he sat by his rainbow river.

Train Trouble

The tiniest train was very excited. After lots of practice, today was the day he would be taking real passengers into town.

The stationmaster picked up his whistle. He had one last word with the tiniest train. "Now, remember," he said, "it's very important to keep to the timetable. Make sure you don't get held up. Whatever happens, keep going! You must reach Hilltown by five minutes past two exactly. Don't be late!"

"I understand," said the tiniest train. "Whoo, whoo! Here we go!"

The stationmaster blew his whistle. The train was off!

There were several passengers on the train already, and the tiniest train was surprised how much harder it was to chug along. Some of them were very big passengers!

As he came to the first station, the tiniest train looked anxiously up at the station clock. What if he was already late? Without hesitating he speeded up, not stopping at the station at all! "I must be on time," he puffed.

So it went on. At each station, the tiniest train was afraid that he was late. He pressed on, not stopping once, remembering what the stationmaster had said.

At last, panting and puffing, he came to Hilltown.

"Goodness me," said the stationmaster there. "I wasn't expecting you for another ten minutes!"

"But it's five minutes to two!" hooted the train.

"And you're due at five minutes past two!" cried the stationmaster. "Just a minute, my phone's ringing!"

It was lots of angry passengers along the way, who had seen the tiniest train dashing past and not been able to get on. There were quite a few cross faces on the train as well – people who had wanted to get off and couldn't!

The stationmaster had a few stern words with the tiniest train. "Passengers don't want a train to be late," he said, "but even a late train is better than no train at all."

This time the tiniest train listened hard. On his next trip he stopped at every station – and he was on time, too!

The Butterfly Ball

Ladybird was scuttling here and there. "Have all the invitations been sent?" she asked Caterpillar.

"Yes," sniffed Caterpillar, "but there wasn't one for *me*!"

"Next year, dear boy," said Ladybird soothingly. "It's butterflies only, I'm afraid, but your turn will come."

Each year the butterfly ball took place late one afternoon in the sunniest part of the border. Ladybird, who loved to be busy, was usually in charge. "Now I must rush," she cried, "to speak to the new butterflies about costumes."

Ladybird flew around the garden. "Remember, dear things," she said to each pair of butterflies she met, "there will be a prize for the loveliest couple as usual. Paint your wings as beautifully as you can. You may win!"

The day of the ball arrived at last. All the creepy-crawlies who were not invited hid under leaves and behind stalks to watch the arrival of the gorgeous butterflies in their painted party costumes. "Ooooh! Aaaaah!" gasped the other insects, as each pair of butterflies looked lovelier than the last. When the dancing began, the sight of dozens of fluttering, jewel-like wings was breathtaking.

Ladybird called for attention. "It is time for the judging of the Most Beautiful Butterfly Couple Contest," she cried. "Ladies and gentlemen, find your partners, please!"

Oh dear, the butterflies were hopelessly mixed up!
Can you help to sort them into their pairs?
And which pair of butterflies do you think should win the prize?

The White World

Bianca couldn't wait for her cousin Bruno to visit, but when he came she began to wish he would go home! Bianca lived in the icy, snowy Arctic. Bruno came from a wooded mountain much further south. His fur was brown, while Bianca's was as white as the world she lived in.

Bruno smiled when he hopped off his iceberg and said hello, but it was the last time. From then on, he moaned without stopping.

"I don't know how you stand it," he grumbled. "I'm used to cold winters, but this is freezing!"

Bianca opened her mouth to explain about her special, warm fur, but Bruno was off again.

"There's nothing to look at," he complained. "Just ice and snow. Where I come from there are trees and mountains, caves and rocks."

Bianca started to explain that polar bears had caves, too, dug out of the ice, but Bruno was still talking.

"No streams!" he groused. "I'm a champion fish-catcher. Look at these claws! How am I going to get any practice in this awful place?"

Bianca began to tell him about fishing through holes in the ice, and the beautiful fish to be found in the cold, deep waters beneath. Bruno would have none of it.

"There's nothing here," he announced, "that isn't better, bigger and more beautiful where I come from. I feel sorry for you, I really do."

Bianca was close to tears. Her mother, who had overheard some of what Bruno was saying looked up at the sky and smiled. "It will be dark in a moment," she said. "Let's sit out here for a moment and enjoy the stars."

"Stars!" snorted Bruno. "Nothing could be more lovely than stars over the mountains in my own land. I don't need to see them."

Suddenly, as happens in the Arctic, night fell. The dark, dark blue sky filled with twinkling points of light. "You see," said Bruno, "just ordinary stars. Oh!"

He sat with his mouth open, gazing up at the pink and red and blue and yellow and green and purple sky. It was the Northern Lights, giving an amazing show, like thousands of fireworks at once.

Bianca and her mother smiled at each other. They knew that there was nothing like this where Bruno came from. As for Bruno, he didn't say a word, which was the second amazing thing that had happened that night!

Ian's Invention

One rainy day, Ian didn't know what to do. "Why don't you make something?" suggested his dad. "You could use that old construction set Uncle Jim gave you."

Ian wasn't very keen at first, but when he had pulled all the pieces out of a battered cardboard box, he started to be interested. There were pipes, and cog-wheels, and elastic bands. There were funnels, and whistles, and axles. There were electric engines, and steam engines, and winding-up mechanisms. There were squiggly bits, and wiggly bits, and bits that looked so strange he wasn't sure *what* they were.

Ian started fitting pieces together. It was fun. Before long, his machine was as big as a chair.

By suppertime, it was bigger still. Ian gathered the family together. "I've invited you," he announced, "to my Grand Switch-On. This is the most remarkable machine the world has ever seen. Prepare to be amazed."

With a flourish, Ian flipped a big red switch. Dad knelt down on the floor for a better view. The dog hid behind Ian's little brother. His sister stepped back and peered over a cupboard door.

Splutter! Wooosh! Carrumph! Gurgle! Google! Whizz! Whir-bang! Eeeeeeeee! The machine began to jiggle. Cogs turned round. Water rushed down pipes and sprayed out in a fountain. Steam puffed out of a big green funnel. A funny hooting sound, like a cow stuck in a bathtub, began to make all the furniture shake.

"What on earth is it?" giggled Dad.

"It's ridiculous!" chortled Ian's sister, wiping tears from her eyes.

Ian's little brother sat down and laughed so hard his glasses fell off.

The dog rolled on the carpet, making a strange wheezing sound.

"But what does it do?" chuckled Dad. "Your machine is a failure, Ian. A machine that does nothing is no good."

But Ian smiled. "Not at all," he said. "My machine has been very successful. It's a Laughter Inducer. You all did laugh, didn't you?"

Waiting for William

Jake's mother told him she had a baby growing in her tummy. "When he comes out, he'll be your little brother," she said.

Jake couldn't wait. Each morning, when he woke up, he ran through to find his parents. "Will it be today?" he asked.

"No, no," said his mother. "Not yet. Growing babies takes a long time."

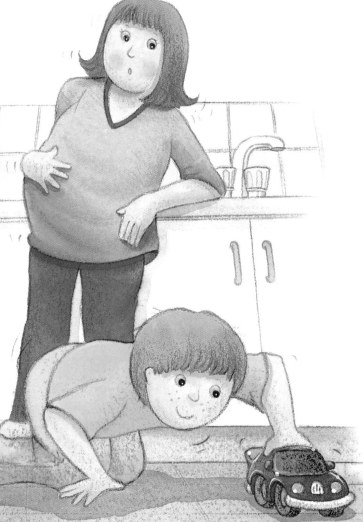

It did seem a very long time to Jake. Then, one morning, when he had almost given up believing in the baby, his mother suddenly said, "Ow! Oh! Jake, I'm going to call Aunty Pat. I think the baby's coming."

Aunty Pat came to look after Jake. Jake's mother walked up and down a lot and took a bath.

"Will it be here soon?" asked Jake.

"No, no," said his mother. "This bit often takes a long time, too."

At suppertime, Dad helped her into the car. "We're going to the hospital," he told Jake.

"But you can't!" wailed Jake. "You need to be here when the baby comes!"

Dad reminded Jake where the baby was! "You'll just have to wait," he said. "I'll ring you as soon as there's news."

Jake didn't want to go to bed, but in the end he was too sleepy to stay awake. "All this waiting makes me tired," he said.

In the morning, Jake woke up to find Aunty Pat sitting on his bed and smiling. "You've got a little brother, Jake," she said. "His name is William."

Jake wanted to go to see William straight away, but Aunty Pat said, "No, we'll wait here. William will be home by lunchtime." So Jake waited some more.

At last, he heard the car arrive. When his mother was settled on the couch, he had a chance to see William for the first time. He was perfect!

"He was worth waiting for," whispered Jake, holding his brother's tiny hand.

"All good things are," smiled his mother.

The Dancing Shoes

"Princess Miranda, it's time for your dancing lesson!" called Madame Evadne. But Princess Miranda had other ideas.

"Dancing is boring," she said. "I don't want to have my lesson today. And I'm a princess, so I don't have to do anything I don't want to!"

Madame Evadne looked cross, but it was true. In Madame Evadne's opinion (well, in everyone in the palace's opinion), Princess Miranda was the rudest, laziest, most spoilt girl in the land, but she was also a princess. Madame Evadne curtseyed and went away.

The same thing soon began to happen whenever Madame Evadne came to teach dancing. As a result, Princess Miranda had no idea how to do the one-step, the two-step, or the Moravian Alpine Fling.

Princess Miranda grew up, as princesses do. And as princesses do, she spotted a prince she thought would make a very good husband.

"Well, there is only one thing to do," said the king, when his daughter told him (she was used to getting what she wanted, remember). "You will have to win his heart at the Royal Ball."

"How?" asked Miranda.

"By dancing like an angel," replied the king, sweeping away.

Princess Miranda looked grim. Then she scurried down into the dungeons where an evil old witch had been kept for several hundred years. The witch was bad but not stupid. In return for her freedom, she gave the princess what she asked for: a pair of magic slippers that would dance divinely all by themselves.

The day of the ball arrived. The prince arrived. Princess Miranda made her entrance. Then the dancing began. Princess Miranda put on the magic slippers and, goodness me, they worked! To everyone's surprise (especially Madame Evadne's), she danced beautifully.

Unfortunately, Miranda had not the slightest idea how to stop the slippers. When the prince asked to take her to supper, she danced on. When she began to feel hungry herself, the slippers wouldn't take her anywhere near the buffet. When she needed to visit the ladies' room, oh dear....

As far as I know, Princess Miranda is still dancing. Two people, though, did find a happy ending. Madame Evadne caught the eye of the prince. The prince caught the eye of Madame Evadne. They lived happily ever after.

Too Many Toys!

"Ooooff!" Jack and Janna's mother landed with a thud. Luckily she fell straight onto the couch in their playroom, but she still wasn't very pleased. "How many times have I told you to put your toys away?" she said, glaring at the truck she had just fallen over. "Christmas is coming, and then there'll be even more toys! What are we to do then?"

Jack and Janna grinned at the idea of Christmas, but they didn't want their mother to get any crosser. "We'll tidy up, we promise," they said, putting on their most angelic expressions.

A few days later, Jack brought a letter home from school. "There's going to be a toy sale," said his mother as she read it. "You can take all the toys you don't play with any more into school. They will be sold on behalf of children who don't have much. That sounds like a good idea to me."

Jack and Janna weren't so sure, but when all their friends began to bring toys into school, they became keener. By the end of the week, they had filled a big cardboard box with toys. Their mother was very happy.

She had a meeting on the day of the toy sale, so Gran came over to keep an eye on the children. "Please can we go to the sale at school, Gran?" asked Jack. "It's in ever such a good cause."

Gran agreed, and when she heard what the money from the sale would be used for, she gave Jack and Janna some extra pocket money to spend as well.

That night, Jack and Janna went to bed with happy smiles. "They've been good as gold," said Gran, when their mother came home. "And you'd be proud of the way they supported the school and poor children today."

"What exactly do you mean?" asked her daughter faintly. "No, I'd better go and see for myself."

It was only just possible to open the door to the playroom. Jack and Janna had bought back nearly all the toys they had taken to the sale … and quite a few more as well.

Gran laughed when she heard what had happened. "At least it's in a good cause," she said. And *everyone* had to agree.

Millie's Magic

Millie was a very sweet little fairy. But she wasn't very good at listening. In the middle of being told something, a dreamy look would come into her eyes.

"What did I just say, Millie?" her mother would ask. And Millie would smile charmingly and say, "I heard every word."

One day, Millie's mother had an appointment. It was a wing check-up. Fairies, you see, have wing check-ups just as we have check-ups for our teeth. It's very important that a fairy's wings work properly, especially if you are a busy mother with a naughty little fairy like Millie to look after.

"I need to wash my wings and get ready," said Millie's mother this particular day. "Could you wash up the lunch things, please? And just do it the human way, please. No magic. You haven't learnt to deal with bubbles yet, and they can be tricky."

Millie promised that she would, but in fact she had stopped listening after the words "wash up the lunch things." As soon as her mother had fluttered upstairs, she climbed onto a chair and said some magic words.

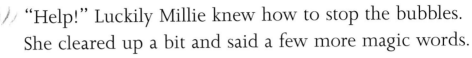

Woooosh! The plates and cups and bowls flew into the sink.

Wheeeee! The tap turned itself on.

Bliggle bloggle bling! Bubbles started to froth up alarmingly over the sink.

"Help!" Luckily Millie knew how to stop the bubbles. She cleared up a bit and said a few more magic words.

Woooosh! The clean plates and cups and bowls jumped out of the sink, twizzled in the air to get dry, and stacked themselves neatly on the table. They gleamed.

Millie clapped her hands with delight and went to get her coat.

A few minutes later, there was a yell from the kitchen.

"Millie!!! Come here at once! What have you done?"

"I just did the washing up," said Millie.

"Isn't there something you've forgotten?" said her mother sharply. "When these dishes were dirty, they had a pattern of stars all over them. Now they're white! You've cleaned off everything, not just the food!"

Millie gasped. It was true. "I can fix it!" she cried.

"Don't even start!" said her mother, but it was too late. In seconds, one plate had a pattern of blue elephants. Another had red stripes. Another had yellow stars.

Do you think Millie's mother put things right? Do *you* always listen carefully?

The Hungry House

One morning, when Mr. Paulus went shopping, he left his front door open. His sister was coming to visit, so he was in a hurry.

Passers-by didn't notice the open door, but the house noticed *them*. It felt hungry. Yes, hungry. Let me explain….

Mr. Paulus was a professor. When he wasn't teaching, he had his nose in a book. Mr. Paulus was always so busy studying, he didn't have any friends. His sister came just once a year.

Mr. Paulus didn't pay attention to his house, either. He kept it clean, but it was years since he had painted it or bought a new carpet. So the house was hungry. It had an empty space inside where there should have been people on the sofas, and paintings on the walls, and delicious smells coming from the kitchen.

So what did the house do, with its door standing open like a big mouth? It ate a passing lady! Then it ate a little boy and his mother. And two grannies with hats on. And the chef from the café opposite. And a dog. After that, the house looked happier.

When Mr. Paulus arrived home, he was surprised to see his front door standing open. He was even more surprised to find that the house seemed somehow more warm and welcoming. He was very, very surprised to find six people and a dog chatting happily in his front room.

"I hope you don't mind," said the chef. "I made us some coffee and found some biscuits. None of us is quite sure how we came here, but we've so enjoyed getting to know each other."

"I brought you some flowers," said one of the grannies. "It was so good of you to invite us, although I can't remember that happening. I put them in a vase for you."

"I put up one of my pictures," said the little boy. "I hope you like it."

"You have a lovely house," said his mother.

Mr. Paulus looked around. It was true! Although he had never noticed in all these years, he did have a lovely house. Just at that moment, his sister arrived.

"Goodness," she said, "what have you done to the place, Albert? It looks wonderful. Oh, hello!"

"Allow me to introduce my friends," said Mr. Paulus, "or … er … perhaps they could introduce themselves."

Mr. Paulus's life changed from that day. He was a much happier man. And his house was much happier, too. Make sure you look after your house, won't you? You never know what a hungry house will do!

They're Behind You!

When Rhiannon went to stay with her aunt, who was a farmer, she couldn't wait to see the animals. She was cross to find that her aunt seemed to want to give her a lecture first!

"You must never feed the animals," said her aunt, "unless I am there. You can really hurt an animal by giving it the wrong food. And you must never drop litter in the fields. Animals can be hurt if they eat that, as well. And you must never go near an animal who has a small baby, unless I am there. The mother might attack you if she thought you were going to hurt her baby."

After a while, Rhiannon stopped listening. She simply wanted to go outside, not listen to all this stuff. That is why she didn't hear the part about never, ever leaving gates open.

At last Rhiannon was free to run out into the farmyard. She went to see the baby pigs first of all. They were so sweet and squiggly that she just had to go inside to say hello. Of course, she completely forgot to shut the gate after her.

The sheep were gorgeous, too. Rhiannon loved the baby lambs and the baby lambs seemed to love her back. Rhiannon skipped out of the meadow like a baby lamb herself – and left the gate open.

The cows were very big and very friendly. They nuzzled up to Rhiannon with their warm breath and big brown eyes. Rhiannon got a little bit frightened and hurried off – leaving the gate open.

Rhiannon also visited the goats, the ducks, and the two little ponies in the back paddock.

At tea time, Rhiannon ran back down the lane to find her aunt.

"It's been great!" she grinned. "You know, all the animals liked me. I've made ever such a lot of friends."

"I know," said her aunt grimly. "They've all followed you home! Look behind you!"

Rhiannon thought it was funny at first, but when her aunt made her give *all* the animals their tea and take them all back to their homes before she had anything to eat herself, she promised should would never, ever leave a gate open again. And she never has.

Leave Those Leaves!

The twins were helping Mamma in the garden. It was a beautiful day, with brown and orange leaves swirling from the trees. Mamma was sweeping leaves off the paths. She had made a big pile beside the shed. It was a terrible temptation to the twins.

"Alfie, don't you dare!" called Mamma, as she spotted her son about to jump into the pile in his red boots.

"No, Mamma," called Alfie.

A moment later, Mamma spotted a little figure in a pink coat shuffling towards the pile. "Angie, I would be very cross!" she cried.

"Yes, Mamma," said Angie.

Faintly, through the window, they all heard the telephone ring in the house.

"I'll only be a minute," said Mamma.

Mamma's minute seemed very long to the twins. They sat on the bench and swung their legs for a while. Angie's boots fell off, but she put them on again. Alfie's boots wouldn't accidentally fall off whatever he tried.

At last, they couldn't bear it any more. "Shall we?" said Alfie.

"Ready, steady, go!" yelled Angie.

Holding hands, they ran towards the pile and jumped right into the middle. Then they tumbled and tossed until they were tired and lay down for a rest.

"Ouch, something's sticking into me," said Angie. She rummaged about. It was Mamma's ring! It must have fallen off as she worked.

The next moment, there was a thunderous rumble and a kind of snorting. "Are you cross, Mamma?" asked Alfie.

Mamma glared down at them. She was just about to give the two a piece of her mind when Angie handed her the ring.

A big struggle went on in Mamma's face. Then she smiled. "It would have been awful to lose this," she said. "Much more awful than clearing up leaves. Now, I must be very careful not to lose this ring again, so I'd better keep my hands in my pockets. Carry on, team!"

Come and Find Me!

Dennis the dinosaur was a very b-i-i-i-g dinosaur. One day, he found his friends Dimple and Dozy playing in the jungle.

"Can I play too?" he asked.

"W-e-l-l," said Dimple doubtfully. "If you like. We're playing hide-and-seek."

"Let me hide! Let me hide!" cried Dennis, jumping up and down and making everything shiver and shake.

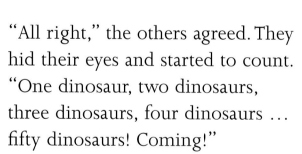

"All right," the others agreed. They hid their eyes and started to count. "One dinosaur, two dinosaurs, three dinosaurs, four dinosaurs … fifty dinosaurs! Coming!"

Oh dear! It really wasn't very hard to find a huge pink and orange dinosaur among the green leaves.

"I don't think this is going to work," said Dozy, when Dennis had been found in one second for the third time.

Even Dennis saw that this was true.
Sadly, he ambled home.

That evening, Dennis didn't eat his
dinner. His mother was worried.
Was her dear son ill? Dennis told
her everything.

Next morning, Dennis's mother took
Dennis and his two friends for a picnic.

"Where are we going?" asked Dimple.

"Somewhere for fun and games,"
replied the largest dinosaur.
"Look! We're here!"

The young dinosaurs played hide-
and-seek all day long. Even Dennis.

Can you find him?

Who's a Pretty Bird?

Most of the time, all the birds who lived at the edge of the forest were great friends. Then, one day, the peacock spread his fine tail and sighed.

"What's the matter?" asked a passing monkey.

"Oh, nothing," said the peacock. "I was just looking at my tail and thinking how very, very beautiful it is."

"What? Not as beautiful as my feathers!" squawked a parrot overhead. "Just look at me! Red, yellow, blue, orange! Far brighter than you, Peacock!"

"Oooh! Rather gaudy, I think," said a gentle voice nearby. "My pure white feathers are much more beautiful." It was a dove, cooing in the branches, who spoke.

Well, the birds carried on arguing all that day and all that night. The other forest animals were kept awake by the noise and were not very pleased.

Next morning, as the birds still squabbled in the trees, the rest of the forest fell silent. Tiger, the fiercest animal of all, had come to see what the fuss was about.

"Well, well," he purred. "This is very useful. After all, a mighty animal like me should only feast on the most beautiful food he can find. When you have decided which of you is the most beautiful, I will be very pleased to eat the winner!"

The birds looked stunned. Then they all spoke at once.

"Some of my feathers are a little faded," said the peacock.

"My feet are not at all attractive," squawked the parrot.

"I'm really a very plain bird," mumbled the dove.

"Then you won't need to argue any more," said the tiger, as he prowled back into the forest. And they never did.

The Racing Snail

One day, a snail and a caterpillar
decided to have a crawling race.

"The caterpillar is quite a bit faster,"
a ladybird told her friend the worm. "There's no doubt that he'll win."

"It depends how long the race is," said the worm.

"Nonsense! What difference would that make?"
The worm gave a little smile and slithered away.

It turned out that the race was very long indeed – right
across the garden and back again. "It will take half the
summer for them to do it," said a grasshopper, "but I'll
bring news back to all the other creepy-crawlies. I could
travel the course in half a dozen hops."

"Ready, steady, crawl!" said a large beetle, and the race began.

Over the days that followed, the grasshopper reported on progress. The snail crept steadily on, but the caterpillar took an early lead and kept it.

Then, one day, the grasshopper jumped back with alarming news for the caterpillar supporters. "He's stopped!" he cried. "He's put on a brown coat and is hanging upside down from a leaf! I expect he needs a little rest."

But the caterpillar carried on sleeping, day after day. One morning, the snail caught up and crawled past him.

The other creepy-crawlies were all waiting on the finish line to cheer home the winner. The snail put on a final sprint, only a leaf's length from the finish. Suddenly, there was a whirring overhead, and a beautiful butterfly fluttered down. "I've won!" cried the caterpillar's unmistakable voice.

The snail took it very well. "I didn't expect to win," he said, "but it was fun trying."

"Actually," said the worm, "you did win. It was a crawling race, and the caterpillar-who-became-a-butterfly flew! Well done, Snail!" And all the creepy-crawlies cheered, even the butterfly.

Bartle's Revenge

There was once a cat called Bartle. He lived with the Cook family. Bartle felt the family did not look after him as he deserved. The children pulled his tail and teased him. Mrs. Cook said he was too fat and cut down his treats. Mr. Cook accused him of leaving yellow patches on the lawn (as if he would!) Granny Cook said he ate her peppermint creams.

One day, Bartle decided he had had enough. He would move in with the lady down the street who always offered him biscuits when he padded past. But first, there was something he needed to do.

He climbed right to the top of the highest tree in the garden and sat there. It took a terribly long time (and a lot of meowing from Bartle) before any of the Cooks realized where he was.

Young Tommy Cook spotted him first. "Don't worry, Bartle, I'm coming to get you," he called, and he set off up the tree.

Soon Tommy was sitting next to Bartle, but he found he couldn't get down again, with or without the cat!

When Caroline Cook spotted Tommy in the tree, she cried out in alarm, "I'll rescue you, Tommy!" and climbed up the tree herself. Soon she was sitting next to her brother, but she, too, found she couldn't get down.

The same thing happened when Matthew Cook climbed the tree, and when Mrs. Cook climbed the tree, and when Mr. Cook climbed the tree. Soon there was a branch full of five Cooks and one Bartle.

"You nincompoops!" called Granny Cook. "Don't panic! I'm coming!"

Granny Cook climbed the tree surprisingly quickly. It took her a little longer to realize that she, too, was stuck.

Bartle smiled in the smug way that only cats can … and calmly strolled down the trunk. He somehow failed to hear the shouts from above, as his mind was on a bag of peppermint creams Granny had under her pillow. It was several hours before neighbours rescued the Cooks. By then, a happy (and fatter) cat was peacefully asleep on the sofa of the lady down the street.

The Clumsy Chameleon

Carlo the chameleon was terribly clumsy. This didn't mean that he dropped things or that he kept falling from branches. There was nothing wrong with his claws at all.

No, Carlo was clumsy with his colouring. As you know, chameleons are very clever at changing how they look so that they match what they are sitting on. That way, other animals looking for a crunchy chameleon snack can't see them.

But Carlo was clumsy. He didn't concentrate. When he was sitting on a brown branch, he would suddenly start daydreaming and find that he had become yellow with stars all over his back.

When he sat on a big grey rock, he would dream again, and turn into a bright red-and-blue-striped chameleon.

"You might just as well yell, 'Come and eat me!'" said his anxious mother. "Really, Carlo, do try to be more careful."

But Carlo simply couldn't keep his mind on the job. The inside of his head was filled with wonderful shapes and colours. Somehow, he just couldn't keep them on the inside. They had to come out.

Carlo's mother consulted Perryman the parrot. He had a reputation for being very wise.

"I know just what you should do," he said. "Get hold of the things on this list for your son. I think you'll find the problem is solved."

So Carlo's mother found smooth sheets of bark, squeezed bright dyes from fruits and seeds, and borrowed some hairs from a friendly warthog.

"Here you are, Carlo," she said, presenting him with the things she had collected, wrapped in a large leaf, "your very own painting set."

Well, no one ever saw Carlo again (though you might if you look very, very carefully), but they certainly saw his ideas and his dreams … in all the wonderful paintings that Carlo created.

Rain, Rain!

Pickle peered out. Green fields stretched far away, with hedges and gates and little lanes in between, but Pickle didn't see any of it. All he could see was the rain. For a little puppy, eager to be outside, that was a horrible sight.

Tom, the little boy who lived at the farm, thought so, too. "Let me take Pickle for a walk, Mamma," he pleaded. "Please!"

But Mamma was firm. "It's too wet, Tom," she said. "No one goes out in weather like this if they can help it."

Pickle barked. "Look!" he woofed. "Those animals are out in the rain!"

A family of thirteen ducks and ducklings was splashing its way happily down the lane.

"Well, those are ducks!" laughed Mamma. "They don't mind the wet!"

"I don't mind the wet either!" wailed Tom. "I love it!"

"Yes, but you haven't got special feathers to keep you warm and keep the wet out," said Mamma.

Pickle looked up with interest. Before anyone could stop him, he ran upstairs and into the biggest bedroom. It was a struggle to open the wardrobe doors, and dresses kept trying to tangle him up, but at last Pickle found what he was looking for. He scuttled downstairs.

"That's my best hat!" yelled Mamma.

"He was just trying to find some feathers to keep us dry," explained Tom, giving Pickle a special cuddle.

"People don't have feathers to keep them dry. They have macs and b…," began Mum, but Pickle and Tom had shot out of the room before she could finish. A minute later, two little figures with big, pleading eyes stood before her, holding waterproofs.

What could Mamma do? Pickle and Tom had a lovely time in the rain, dashing and splashing and chasing … the ducks!

Around the World

When Terence the turtle decided to swim around the world, his family and friends laughed.

"Don't be ridiculous!" chortled Papa Turtle. "The world is very big. At least, I've heard it is. And you are very small. You'd never make it."

"You're not even as good a swimmer as me!" crowed his sister Teresa.

"Don't be daft, lad," said Grandad.

But Terence was determined. One sunny morning, he said goodbye to his friends and relations and swam bravely off into the ocean.

He hadn't gone very far before he began to get tired. He could still see the beach where his sister and mother were sunning themselves. Perhaps this hadn't been such a good idea after all.

Two hours later, Terence was very, very tired. His flippers trailed in the water. He was pretty sure he didn't even have the strength to swim back to the beach.

"I've been very, very silly," sighed Terence. He began to sink lower in the deep, deep water.

Suddenly, *woooosh!* Terence felt himself flying up in the air. He somersaulted in the sunshine and fell back down … onto the back of a passing whale!

"Oh, sorry," said the whale, in a deep, musical voice. "Shall I shake you off?"

"No, no!" gasped Terence. "I was just about to sink." He told the whale the whole story.

"As it happens," said the whale carelessly, "I'm just off around the world myself. Would you like to come too?"

Terence gasped. It was a dream come true. So the little turtle and his new friend set off around the world. They had a wonderful time.

A year later, a tired but happy turtle scrambled up onto a familiar beach.

"Jumping jellyfish!" cried his father. "You did it!"

"Was it hard, darling? Was it dangerous?" asked his mother, anxiously.

Terence just smiled. "Oh no," he said. "I had a whale of a time!"

Guess Who!

"Goodness me, Willy! Stop getting under my paws!" growled Mother Wolf one morning. "Why can't you go out and play in the forest like other wolves? But remember, be back in time for lunch and don't talk to any strange humans."

Willy lolloped off into the forest. He was bored. Then, ahead, he saw something red among the trees. It was a little girl.

Now Willy knew he wasn't supposed to talk to strangers, but he didn't think there would be any harm in smiling and waving.

The little girl frowned. "I can't stop to talk to you," she said fiercely. "I'm going to my granny's house. Go away!"

Willy was frightened. Humans really were fierce! He ran off through the trees.

Panting, and feeling that he couldn't run any further, he suddenly came to a clearing with a little cottage. A very, very tasty smell was coming from it. Willy slunk forward and put his nose around the open door.

Inside, a little old lady was putting clothes away in a cupboard. Willy bounded over to do more smiling and waving, but the cottage was small, and he bounded a bit too bouncily. *Bang!* He fell against the cupboard door, which shut tight … with the little old lady inside!

Just then, a familiar voice called out. "Granny! Granny!"

Willy looked around wildly. There was nowhere to hide. Then he had an idea. He jumped into the bed and pulled the covers up to his chin.

The little girl came up to the bed. "Why, Granny," she said crossly, "you look terrible. Your eyes are red. Your ears are dirty! And *when* did you last clean your teeth?"

She peered more closely at Willy. With a shriek, he jumped out of the bed and ran from the cottage, home to the rabbit pie his dear old mother had made for lunch.

"I'll never go near a human being again," he promised her. "I was only trying to be friendly, but they're horrible!"

"Quite right, son," said his mother. And they lived happily ever after.

The Sneaky Snake

There was once a snake who longed more than anything to be a secret agent. The jungle animals were surprised and amused when he told them.

"You have to be good at codes," said the tree frog.

"I am," said the snake. "I've been studying. %*+^>*! See?"

The other animals didn't know what that meant, but they didn't like to say so. "All right, but you have to be good at spotting clues," said the parrot.

"I am," replied the snake. "I can tell that you had blueberries for breakfast."

"That's amazing!" squawked the parrot, not realizing that he had blueberry juice all round his beak.

"Hah!" said the monkey. "You also have to be a master of disguise! How can a snake look like another animal? You don't have any legs, for a start."

The snake smiled a secret smile. "I bet I'm better at disguise than you imagine," he said. "Let's test it. I'll go off into the jungle and return in disguise. You can tell each other secrets. Later, I'll tell you what they all were, to prove I was there."

The animals agreed. "He couldn't possibly dress up as a monkey," said the monkey.

"Or a frog," said the tree frog.

"I'd like to see him fly!" scoffed the parrot.

That afternoon, the animals gathered in the middle of a flower-filled clearing and shared their secrets. They kept their voices low and were as sure as they could be that no one could overhear them.

You can imagine how surprised they were when the snake came slithering back in the early evening. "So your middle name is Polly?" he greeted the parrot. "And you don't like water, Tree Frog? And you want to be an astronaut, Monkey?" He knew all their secrets!

The animals had to agree that the snake was a super sneaky secret agent. They never did find out how he disguised himself. Could you tell them?

The Singing Bird

There was once a man who was very poor. He couldn't afford a comfortable house or delicious food and drink. Every day, he got up, ate a crust of bread, and worked hard until bedtime.

But there was one thing that made him happy, and he didn't have to pay a penny for it. Outside his window, a little bird sang him awake in the morning and sang him to sleep at night. She had a beautiful song. The man felt that as long as he could hear the song of the bird, he could go on.

One day, something amazing happened. The man had a letter to say that his great uncle had died and left him a huge amount of money. The man hadn't even known that he *had* a great uncle, so the news came as a great shock.

Of course, the man's life changed overnight. He went straight out and bought himself a beautiful house in the mountains. He didn't even bother to pack up his few poor possessions, but there was one thing he couldn't leave behind. He bought a golden cage and put the singing bird in it.

"You can come and sing to me," he said, "just as you did before. You are the only thing from my old life that was beautiful, and you are beautiful still."

But when the bird in the golden cage arrived at the luxurious new house, she refused to sing. Nothing the man did would make her open her beak.

"It must be because you are in a cage," said the man. "I'm sorry. Sit on this branch outside my window and sing to me there. I know you won't fly away."

Well, the bird didn't fly away, but she didn't sing, either. She was silent and sad all day long.

Gradually, the man realized that he was sad, too. He had money, fine clothes and delicious food, but he didn't have the one thing he wanted most in the world.

"I know what you want, little bird," he whispered one day. "You want to go home, and so do I." He placed the bird gently on his shoulder and, leaving all his fine things behind, walked back to his old house.

The sun was going down as he arrived. With a sigh, the man lay down on his hard bed and closed his eyes. Outside, the beautiful voice of the bird broke into song, and the man smiled.

"I was rich all along," he said, "I just didn't know it."

The Tall Tree

Long ago and far away there was a jungle. A hot, steamy jungle. And in the middle of the jungle was a huge tree. And on this tree grew the most delicious fruit in the world. All the animals loved it. It tasted like strawberries and apples and bananas and oranges all mixed up together.

One day, a little monkey, sitting on a branch and munching one of the yummy fruits, noticed something important. There was only one fruit left. It was right at the top of the tree. He hurried to tell the other animals.

"Goodness me," said the monkey's mother. "Your father and I had better eat that fruit. Just to stop it falling into the wrong hands, you know."

"Actually, it should be mine," said a mouse. "I have ten little babies to feed. Our need is greater than yours."

"Well," said the tiger, "I am the fiercest animal in the jungle, so I will obviously be the one to eat the last fruit. Just you try and stop me!"

Suddenly the parrot laughed out loud.

"And how are any of you going to reach the fruit?" she asked. "Can you climb so high, Tiger? No? Or you, Mouse? No? And what about you, Mother Monkey? I know you can climb high, but can you climb as high as that?"

The monkey was forced to confess that she could not.

"Only a bird can reach that fruit," squawked the parrot. "And I am going to do it right now!"

The parrot flew up, up, up to the gleaming fruit. She pecked with her sharp beak … and suddenly gave a squawk. The fruit was so big and heavy that it slipped through her claws. The animals watched, open-mouthed, as the fruit fell down, down, down and hit the ground with a thud! It smashed into such tiny pieces that there was not the smallest crumb for anyone to eat.

"It's a disaster!" cried the monkey. But she was wrong. When the fruit hit the ground, hundreds of tiny seeds flew out into the jungle. In the steamy heat, they soon grew … and a whole forest of fruit trees kept all the animals happy!

A House for Mouse

Mouse lived in a snug little house he had built himself. It nestled between the roots of a hawthorn tree. He was happy there.

One day, when Mouse was out gathering berries, the farmer decided to cut the long grass at the edge of the field, and Mouse's house disappeared.

Mouse was very upset. It was late in the year. Bad weather was coming. How would he manage in the winter without a house? Mouse packed some seeds and berries into a little basket and set off to find somewhere new to live.

A mouse is very small. He doesn't need a huge house. Mouse thought it would be easy to find a snug little place. He was wrong.

"This flowerpot looks perfect," said Mouse.

"It is perfect for me!" croaked a big brown toad.

"I could be cosy in the hole in this tree," squeaked Mouse.

"Not with me inside!" hooted a fierce-looking owl.

"I would be quite comfortable under this old shed," cried Mouse.

"Really?" asked a very large rat.

Poor Mouse tramped on for days. He soon ate his seeds and berries. He felt tired and hungry. Each night, the wind blew colder.

Then, one clear day, Mouse was scuttling along when he almost fell into the most beautiful little mouse's house he had ever seen. It reminded him of his own dear home, now gone for ever.

"This is just right for a mouse," said Mouse, "but it is so well cared for, someone must already live here."

"Yes," said a voice, "I do. But it is very lonely all by myself."

Mouse looked up into the bright little eyes of a smiling mouse who looked just like him – except that she was a lady mouse.

So that is how Mouse found a home and a wife all in one day. Years later, when his grandchildren had little bumps and bruises, he would say, "You know, losing my home was the best thing that ever happened to me. You just never know when something bad is going to turn into something very, very good."

Shhhh!

Marco was having a wonderful birthday party. All his friends were there. But the moment he was dreading had nearly arrived. In came Marco's mother, proudly carrying a huge banana-frosted birthday cake. (Marco loved bananas.)

Marco looked up at his mother as she put the cake on the table. "Please don't sing, Mamma," he whispered. "P-l-e-a-s-e!"

It was too late. She had already started on "Happy Birthday," only it was more like

"Happy Birthday!"

You see, Marco's mother had a really, really loud voice. Whenever she sang, Marco was sooooo embarrassed.

A few days later, Marco and his mother went on a camping trip with four of his best friends. Before they went, Marco made his mother promise that no matter how many campfire songs they sang, or how many Tarzan yells they called, she would never, ever join in.

The camping trip was fun, and Marco's mother kept her word, though she sometimes had to put her paws over her mouth.

On the last day, the friends (and Marco's mother) hiked through the woods to a deserted canyon. It was a fantastic day … until they reached the canyon. Just as they all safely got to the bottom, rocks began tumbling down above them. Marco's mother hurried the little ones to safety, but the damage was done. The only path up the steep sides was blocked. There was no way out.

"Help!" shouted Marco and his friends. "Help! Help! Help!" Their voices sounded tiny. No one came. Marco looked at his mother. She nodded.

  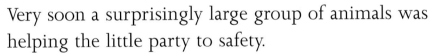

"Help!" she thundered. "HELP!"

Very soon a surprisingly large group of animals was helping the little party to safety.

"I suppose it's quite useful, sometimes, having a loud voice," sighed Marco, as they tramped home.

"Can be," grunted Mamma.

"Doesn't mean you have to use it every day," said Marco casually.

"Say no more, Marco," grinned Mamma. "Emergencies only from now on!"

Mr. Noah's Problem

When Mr. Noah built the ark, he thought carefully about where all the animals would sleep. He made big stalls for the elephants and the hippos. He put a window in the roof of the giraffes' stall, so that they didn't get cricks in their necks. He made homes in little boxes for the mice and the hamsters, so that the bigger animals wouldn't stand on them by mistake.

"I really think I've thought of everything," Mr. Noah told his wife, as he watched dark storm clouds gather overhead. Mrs. Noah wasn't so sure. "What about the woodworms?" she asked.

"All taken care of," said Mr. Noah happily. "There will be plenty of room for them in the box I have made for the earwigs and the fleas."

"And what is the box made of?" asked Mrs. Noah quietly.

"Well, wood, of course!" cried Mr. Noah. Then he frowned and said, "Oh!"

"Exactly," said Mrs. Noah. She had realized that the ark, and everything in it, was made of wood. And woodworms eat wood. They make lots of little holes as they munch their way through planks and beams. And sooner or later, lots of little holes might let in water.

Mr. Noah thought hard. Then he went into his workshop and made lots of little wooden balls. "Now I must talk to the woodworms," he said.

The next day, the rain came down. It rained for forty days and forty nights. Everyone was overjoyed when it stopped at last, and the ark came to rest on the top of a mountain.

"Well done, Mr. Noah!" said his wife, giving him a hug.

"No, without you, it could have been a disaster," said Mr. Noah. "My friends and I have a present for you to say thank you." He gave a delighted Mrs. Noah a beautiful necklace of wooden beads. Each one had a tiny, perfect hole munched all the way through it for the string. I wonder how that happened…?

The Outsider

Ferdinand was a small fish. He lived near a coral reef, where the water was warm and blue. All around him swam bright little fish of every kind you can imagine. There were orange ones with yellow stripes. There were green ones with blue spots. There were red fish and purple fish and yellow fish.

But Ferdinand wasn't patterned. He didn't have long, flowing fins. He couldn't jump out of the water like the flying fish. There was nothing very interesting about him at all. He was a sludgy brown colour, and most of the time, no one noticed him.

"Everyone can't be flashy," said his mother. "You're fine as you are, Ferdy."

Ferdinand wasn't so sure. He wanted to be noticed. He tried to improve the way he looked by draping bits of seaweed around himself. It wasn't a great success. In fact, it made it even harder to spot him.

Sometimes, the other fish made fun of Ferdinand. "Oops, sorry, Ferdy," they would say, as they bumped into him. "We didn't see you there. We thought you were a patch of mud! Ha ha!"

Then, one day, as Ferdinand was lurking near a sludgy brown rock, there was a great splashing and thrashing in the water nearby. Ferdy saw some gleaming white teeth and a bright, beady eye. Luckily, the bright, beady eye didn't see him. It did see the orange fish with yellow stripes. It did see the green fish with blue spots. It saw the red fish and the purple fish and the yellow fish, too.

And it ate them all up in a single shark-sized gulp.

When the shark had eaten everyone in sight, she swam slowly off in search of another snack. Ferdy floated gently out of his hiding place and looked around. He decided that if he had to choose between being a sludgy brown fish outside a shark or a bright, flashy fish inside a shark, he knew exactly what he thought was best. And he swam home to tell his mother.

A Roaring Success

Len and Laura Lion were very proud parents. They called their first cub Leo and showed him off to all their friends.

"He's going to take after his old dad," said Len, puffing out his chest. "He'll be the raciest runner and the most powerful pouncer in the pride. And he'll probably have my magnificent mane, too."

"I'm fine, Dad," said Leo. And he was. He just wasn't the racing, pouncing champion Len had hoped for.

"Leave the boy alone," said Laura. "He's a great cub. And his mane is starting to grow. Who knows?"

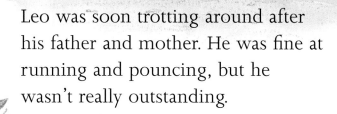

Leo was soon trotting around after his father and mother. He was fine at running and pouncing, but he wasn't really outstanding.

"Are you trying, son?" asked Len, when Leo trailed in last after a practice run. "The other cubs were miles ahead. What's the trouble? Thorn in the paw? Sniffles in the nose? You can tell me."

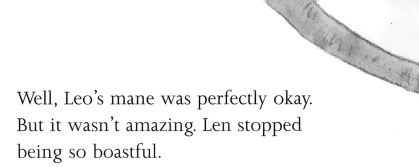

Well, Leo's mane was perfectly okay. But it wasn't amazing. Len stopped being so boastful.

Then, one day, when the older lions were out hunting, a pack of hyenas came sniffing around the clump of grass where the baby cubs and bigger young lions like Leo were resting.

At once, the nearly-grown-up lions sprang to their feet, pouncing and snarling. The hyenas took no notice. They had spotted a plump little cub in the grass. Closer and closer they came, until some of the young lions let out roars to frighten them away. They had never had to use their roars before. It did no good. Then, suddenly…

ROOoaAAaaaRRrrr!

It was Leo! The whole savannah shook at the sound. The hyenas ran off, and the grown-up lions came running back as they heard the noise.

Everyone agreed. A roar like that had never been heard before. Leo was a star at last. And Len? He is a very happy lion indeed.

Bess's Busy Day

One fine morning, Farmer Phil set off to plough the North Field.

"I won't need you today, Bess," he called to his sheepdog. "You can keep an eye on the barnyard for me."

Bess looked a little lost. She felt that her proper place was just behind Farmer Phil's left boot, or rounding up the sheep out on the hills. Then, with a small sigh, she settled down in the sun for a snooze.

But sheepdogs are busy dogs. They like to be active. When, a couple of minutes later, Doris Duck waddled past with her brood of five ducklings, Bess couldn't resist it. She jumped to her feet and began to round up those ducklings into what she thought was a more orderly line.

Doris was not pleased. "Leave my ducklings alone!" she quacked. "You're frightening them! They can walk perfectly well by themselves, thank you!"

116

Bess lay down again. She had only just settled her nose on her front paws when, out of the corner of her eye, she spotted a couple of Henny Hen's chicks wandering about near the barn door. At once, Bess rushed over to shoo them back to the henhouse.

"Do you mind?" squawked Henny. "I'm trying to teach my chicks where everything is in the barnyard. If I wanted them to be in the henhouse, I'd shoo them there myself!"

Poor Bess! She tried to keep the piglets out of the mud, but Pedro Pig got cross. She chased the mice around the barn, until Pom the cat told her that was *his* job.

When farmer Phil came back from the fields, the farmyard was in uproar. All the animals were squawking and clucking and quacking and squeaking and squealing at once.

Farmer Phil couldn't understand it, until he saw Bess sitting with her head between her paws and looking sorry for herself.

"Don't worry, old girl," he said. "I should have remembered. You're not a guard dog, you're a *working* dog. Next time, you come with me, where you belong."

And the whole farmyard cheered!

Ten Little Frogs

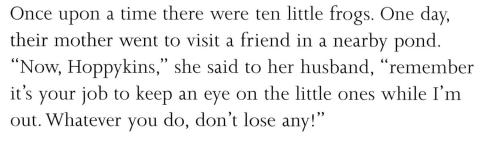

Once upon a time there were ten little frogs. One day, their mother went to visit a friend in a nearby pond. "Now, Hoppykins," she said to her husband, "remember it's your job to keep an eye on the little ones while I'm out. Whatever you do, don't lose any!"

"Yes, dear," said Hoppy. But those froglets were lively. They jumped about all over the place. Before long, Hoppy was hot and bothered.

"One, two, three, four … oh no, I've counted you twice," he began. "One, two, three, four, five, six, eight, nine, ten. Hang on, I've got one left!"

Hoppy did his best to make the little frogs behave. He lined them all up on a log and began to count. "One, two, three, four, five, six, seven, eight, nine, ten, eleven, twelve, thirteen … what?"

Hoppy didn't notice that the frog at the beginning kept jumping to the end, ready to be counted all over again.

Hoppy told the frogs to jump into the pond to cool down. Actually, it was Hoppy who needed to cool down. But in the water, it was even harder to keep track of them.

All too soon, the sound that Hoppy had been dreading boomed through the water. "Hoppykins! I'M HOME!"

Poor old Hoppy looked glum. He knew he was in for a telling-off. But the froglets knew their mother, too. And they guessed that if their dad got a piece of her mind, they would, too. So one by one, they came creeping out. Can you spot them before their mother does?

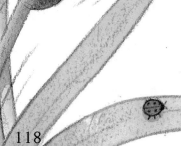

Quarrrk!

It was midnight in the jungle. All the animals were asleep. Monkey was snug in his nest of leaves. Parrot was perched on his sleeping branch. Snake was curled round the trunk of a tree. Lizard snored nearby. And far below, Tiger and his cubs slept peacefully on the forest floor.

Suddenly, "Quarrrk! Quarrrk!"

Everyone jumped up at the awful sound. Tiger growled and stood in front of his cubs. Lizard scampered out of sight. Snake hissed warningly. Parrot flew up, scattering feathers, and Monkey chattered with fright.

"W-w-w-w-what was that?"

Everything was quiet. The animals listened. They couldn't hear anything other than the usual rustling jungle sounds. One by one, they drifted off to sleep again. Until…

"Quarrrk! Quarrrk!"

This time, Tiger was angry. "Who's making that noise?"

But still, nothing stirred in the jungle. Once again, the animals settled down.

When the horrible noise happened for the third time, Tiger decided to act. "One of us must stay awake," he snarled, "to see who is disturbing our sleep. If this is some kind of joke, Monkey, it's not a very good one."

"It's n-n-not me!" chattered Monkey. "I'll stay awake and listen. You'll see."

So the other animals went back to sleep, and Monkey rubbed his eyes to keep awake.

"Quarrrk!" Thud!

Monkey fell off his branch and landed on Tiger!

"It was right in my ear!" gasped Monkey.

"Which ear?" asked Tiger.

"This ear!" screeched Monkey. "It was scary."

Tiger stared up at the branches above. "The squawking animal nearest your right ear, Monkey, was Parrot," he growled.

"I didn't do it!" squawked Parrot.

"I'm afraid you did, old friend," said Tiger kindly. "You've been sleeptalking! And I've got the answer." He tied a vine around Parrot's beak in a neat bow.

"I'll take it off in the morning," he said. "Sweet dreams, everyone!"

And that's exactly what they had.

No Place Like Home

Pauly was a polar bear. He lived with his mother in an ice cave near the North Pole. Even if he walked all day, all he could ever see was ice and the cold sea of the Arctic Ocean.

As he grew older, Pauly began to think that perhaps there might be more to life than ice and sea. He chatted to the gulls who flew overhead and heard tell of lands that were green, not white, and seas that were warm and full of bright little fish. More and more, Pauly longed to see them.

One day, a new seabird flew in to land near Pauly's cave. He didn't look like the other gulls and, when Pauly told him of his dreams, he said an extraordinary thing. "Well, that's no problem," he chirped. "I can do magic, you see."

In a flash, Pauly found himself sitting next to the bird in a completely different place! There was sand under his paws, and palm trees ran along the shore of the bluest sea he had ever seen.

"What do you think?" asked the bird.

"It's beautiful," said Pauly. "But the brightness hurts my eyes. And, oh dear, it is so hot!"

"No problem!" said the bird. In a flash, Pauly found himself in a cooler place. Everywhere he looked there was green grass, and lots of fences, between which animals strolled and munched the grass.

"It's a farm," said the bird. "Is this better?"

"Those poor animals!" cried Pauly. "They can't go wherever they like! And, oh dear, it is still so hot!"

Before he had finished speaking, Pauly found himself in yet another place. Tall, tall trees towered overhead, while a little stream sparkled by his feet. The air in the forest smelt damp and cool.

"I'm sorry," whispered Pauly, "but I still don't like it. What if those trees fell on me? And, oh dear, even here it is so hot!"

In the blink of an eye, Pauly found himself back in his old home. He sniffed the cold air and dug his paws into the icy snow.

"I hope you're happy!" chirped the bird. "I can't believe you prefer this to the wonders of the world I have shown you."

"But I do," smiled Pauly. As he fell asleep, the rainbow colours of the Northern Lights shimmered overhead. "Home is always the most wonderful place in the world," whispered one happy little bear.

The Tiny Friend

Long ago, a huge, hairy mammoth stomped through a forest in search of food. Although he looked scary, he was really very gentle and kind. He ate leaves and grass, but he needed a lot of both. That was why he was always on the move, trying to fill his rumbling tummy.

One day, as the mammoth was munching a bush of leaves and berries, he heard a very tiny sound and felt a tickling in his ear. He shook his head impatiently from side to side, but the sound and the tickling went on. When he kept still, the mammoth could hear that the sound was a very tiny voice.

"Please," said the voice, "oh, please, Mammoth, don't put your great foot down. My little ones are just underneath."

The mammoth looked down. He had been resting one foot on a small rock, and there, just where he was about to put his foot, lots of tiny spiders were running about.

"Please don't hurt them," begged the mother spider, who was hanging from a thread near the mammoth's mighty ear.

The mammoth was, as I said, kind. So he carefully plodded away, being careful not to put his great feet on any tiny creatures.

A few days later, as he was wandering through the forest, the mammoth heard something that frightened him very much. It was a shout. The mammoth knew that human beings liked to hunt mammoths with their sharp spears. As quickly as he could, he trotted away, the ground shaking at every step.

But the human hunters were faster. Before long, the mammoth felt spears whistling past his ears. And the shouts grew louder and fiercer. He ran forward, and squeezed through the opening of a large cave. At first it seemed a good hiding place, but as the hunters grew nearer, the mammoth realized that he was trapped. There was no other way out of the cave. He would be found for sure.

"Don't worry," said a voice that he could hardly hear above the sound of his thumping heart.

"You did me a kindness. Now I will help you."

At an amazing speed, the spider spun a web across the entrance to the cave. When the hunters arrived, they shook their heads. "He can't be in here," they grunted. "This cobweb hasn't been disturbed."

Slowly, their shouts disappeared into the distance. "Thank you," breathed the mammoth, but his little friend had gone, and the huge animal never heard his tiny voice again.

Hide-and-seek

Once upon a time there were ten little bugs:

Una, Tula, Trina, Forster, Quentin,

Cicely, Septimus, Otto, Nina and Declan.

They lived with their mother in a beautiful garden.

One day, the mother bug said to her little ones, "Sweethearts, I must fly off and see how the roses at the other end of the garden are doing. You ten stay right here under this leaf. I won't be long."

The little bugs hadn't been sitting still for long before it started to rain. Water dripped from their leaf and fell … splosh! … on the ground. When it stopped at last, the sun came out. The whole garden glittered with jewel-like raindrops.

"It looks lovely," gasped Una. "Let's go and explore."
Without thinking for a minute about what their mother
had said, the naughty little bugs set off.

Some liked yellow flowers best and jumped onto their
sunshiny petals. Others headed for blue flowers,
sparkling and nodding. Otto spotted some bright red
dahlias and could hardly be seen, as she was red, too!
Two little bugs had fun sliding down the day-lily leaves.

When their mother came back a few minutes later, she
was horrified to find her babies gone. She guessed what
had happened but she knew that she had to find her
little ones quickly, before a hungry bird spotted them!
"It will take me ages to find them all among the
flowers," she sighed. "I hardly know where to start."
Do you think you could help her?

The last little bug of all was the hardest to find. At last
the adventurer was found under an upturned flowerpot.
Can you work out which one that was?

The Secret Pet

One afternoon, when Benjamin was walking home from school, he saw a scruffy little puppy sitting on the pavement. As he passed, the puppy put its head on one side and looked up appealingly.

"Sorry, mate," said Benjamin. "My mother won't even let me think about having a pet. And my dad's worse."

The puppy gave a little whine, as if to show that it understood.

Benjamin walked on, but when he paused to cross the road opposite his house, he noticed that a scruffy little puppy was sitting just behind him.

"No, no," said Benjamin, squatting down to talk to the puppy. "I meant it. You really can't come home with me. My parents would never let me keep you. They'd probably take you to the Dogs' Home."

The puppy looked at the pavement. Reluctantly, Benjamin picked up his book bag and carefully crossed the road, deliberately not looking behind him.

Over supper, Benjamin was very quiet. He couldn't help thinking about the puppy.

"Are you all right, Ben?" asked his dad. "You've hardly touched your pizza."

Benjamin didn't think it would be a good idea to mention the puppy, so he just said he wasn't very hungry.

Later, when he got ready for bed, Benjamin went to the window and pulled the curtains. Outside on the pavement, sitting in the pool of light from a streetlamp, sat a familiar figure.

All night long, Benjamin tossed and turned. It was no good. At half past three, when the house was quiet, he crept downside and carried the little dog inside.

"Just for tonight," he whispered, "and don't make a sound."

The puppy was as good as gold. He settled down on the rug beside Benjamin's bed and went to sleep.

An hour later, the whole house was woken by a terrible noise. Downstairs, what sounded like a very big dog was barking at the top of his voice. The whole family rushed downstairs to find a small, scruffy puppy pinning a shifty looking character to the sofa.

It was breakfast time before the police had carted away the burglar, and the puppy had been explained.

"Now, Ben," said his dad, "you know we've always said no pets. Your mother and I are just not keen on the idea."

Ben looked sad.

"Of course," said Dad, "guard dogs are a different matter entirely!"

Oswald Learns a Lesson

Oswald Ostrich was a very clever little bird. When I say that he was little, I mean that his mother and father towered over him, but compared with most birds of his age, Oswald was HUGE!

Oswald lived on a dusty plain. There were one or two bare-looking trees but nothing else at all for miles and miles. The animals that lived on the plain were always on the move, usually in groups with their friends and families.

Oswald was always eager for new ideas and information to fill his clever little head, so he made friends with all the animals he met. By talking to the other animals, Oswald learnt a great many things. The gazelles showed him how to play jumping games. The lions showed him how to creep up on gazelles (just to surprise them, of course). Oswald was keen to try everything.

Then, one day, Oswald met a vulture. He was an ugly bird, and Oswald was a little frightened of him at first, but it turned out that Vic, as he was called, knew a great many interesting things. Oswald never tired of hearing about all the amazing adventures Vic had had as he flew across Africa.

"Tell me more about flying," said Oswald. "Could anyone do it?"

"No, no," laughed Vic hoarsely. "Gazelles can't do it. Lions can't do it. You have to be a bird to do it."

Oswald flapped his own stubby wings. Nothing happened. He tried running very fast and flapping his wings. Still nothing happened. He tried running even faster, until even the startled gazelles were left behind, but his funny little feet never left the ground.

His dad found him sad and exhausted, flopped against a tree.

"There's something wrong with me," said Oswald. "I'm a bird but I can't fly. I'm so sorry, Dad."

Dad grinned. "Have you ever seen me fly, Oswald?" he asked. "No? Well that's because ostriches are very, very special birds. We never fly. In fact, we're very strict about it. Let chattering parrots and smelly vultures fly. We don't need to."

"Why not?" asked Oswald.

"Because we can run!" cried his Dad. "We can run faster than any bird in the world! Why would we want to fly? Come on, you're a big boy now, I'll race you back."

And after all his take-off practice, Oswald was so fast he even beat his dad. He decided that he had a lot to be proud about after all.

131

The Cat and the Dog

Once there was a cat called Cuddles and a dog called Major. They both lived with Arianna Detrop, the famous opera singer, but they were not friends. Cuddles thought that Major was big and rough with no manners. Major thought that Cuddles was a foolish, fluffy animal who lolled about on silk cushions all day, (which, in truth, he did.)

Arianna Detrop was away a great deal. The animals hardly saw her. They spent most of their time apart or sitting with their backs to each other in front of the fire.

One day, a dreadful thing happened. During one of her most powerful performances, in the middle of a "*Tra-la-la-LA!*", Madame Detrop fell off the stage! She broke her leg and had to come home to rest.

Things changed overnight for Cuddles and Major …
and not for the better. For Major, the problem was the
singing. Madame Detrop was so keen to keep her voice
in trim while she was at home that she sang every
moment of the day. It was loud singing. Very loud singing.
Poor Major put his paws over his ears and whined softly.
He had never been so miserable.

Cuddles had a different problem. Like many white
cats, he couldn't hear very well, so he wasn't worried
about the singing, but he was bothered by the *sitting*.
It didn't matter which cushion he chose for a
comfortable snooze, Madame Detrop always decided
to sit on that one herself.

Stuck at home with no exercise, Madame had been
tucking into chocolates sent by admirers. Her bottom
was not small. On several occasions, Cuddles was
almost squashed flat.

One evening, when Madame was tirra-lirra-ing from the sofa,
Major and Cuddles met on the stairs. For the first time,
they did not view each other as enemies.

"I have an idea that might solve both our problems,"
woofed Major hesitantly. "But you might
not like it." He whispered in Cuddles's ear.

"It's purrrrfect!" smiled Cuddles.

So Major found some fantastic earmuffs,
and Cuddles found a comfortable place
to snooze. They were friends at last.

133

The Lost Quack

It was a beautiful rainy day at the pond. *Splish! Splash! Splosh!* went the raindrops in the water. *Quack! Quack! Quack!* said the ducks. *Croak! Croak! Croak!* called the frogs. They all loved the rain.

"Isn't it lovely, darlings?" a mother duck on the bank quacked to her five little ducklings, who hadn't seen rain before.

"*Quack!*" agreed the first duckling.

"*Quack!*" agreed the second.

"*Quack! Quack!*" cried the next two.

"*Croak!*" said the fifth, and was so surprised that he fell into the water in a flurry of feathers.

Mother Duck watched anxiously as he bobbed to the surface and clambered back onto the bank.

"Are you all right?" she quacked.

"*Croak!*" said the little duckling. "When I open my beak, that's the noise that comes out. Yesterday it was a quack and today it's a croak."

"I don't like this at all," said his mother. "We'll ask Queen Swan."

The beautiful white bird was thought to be very wise. She listened carefully to what the mother duck said.

"It sounds to me," said Queen Swan, "as if someone has stolen your quack and given you a croak instead. All you need to do is to find out who is now quacking when they should be croaking."

"You mean it's one of those frisky frogs?" quacked Mother Duck. "I should have known. Leave it to me, Your Majesty. I'll soon have this sorted out."

Mother Duck knew that if she asked the frogs to croak one by one, they would be awkward and hide in the weeds. She thought of a plan.

"This afternoon," she said, "we are having a singing competition. Please line up if you want to take part. Frogs first!"

All the frogs, who were proud of their singing voices, lined up on the bank.

"Now, first I want to hear how loudly you can sing," said the mother duck. "One croak each, please, in turn. One, two, three…!"

Croak, croak, croak, croak … the frogs began … croak, croak, croak, CROAK, CROAK, CROAK, QUACK!

"Aha!" Mother Duck scooped the offending frog up under her wing and dragged him off to find her duckling.

"You just give him his quack back right away," she said firmly.

"It was just a joke," said the frog. "A croak joke." But he did what she asked. The little duckling was happy to be quacking once more. And even the naughty frog was pleased, because after all that, he won the singing competition!

The Egg Hunt

Oona the hen laid a beautiful brown egg every single day. She was proud of her eggs and looked forward to sitting comfortably on them for a few weeks until they hatched out into dear little fluffy chickens.

But Oona had a problem. Each day, as soon as she had laid one perfect, brown egg, the farmer came along and took it away. You see, he loved Oona's eggs for his breakfast. There never were any eggs left for Oona to sit on.

Oona was not a clever hen, but at last it dawned on her that she must do something. The answer, she knew, was to hide her eggs.

The next day, she didn't lay her egg in the henhouse. She laid it under the hedge in a nice quiet spot.

It took the farmer ten minutes to find the egg he was sure must be somewhere about.

The next day, Oona laid in the barn, high up on a bale of straw. Even so, the farmer found the egg after hunting for fifteen minutes.

And so it went on. Each day, Oona laid an egg. And each day, the farmer hunted and hunted until he found it. This happened for weeks and weeks. One day, it took the farmer all morning to find the egg, and he wasn't very pleased to have to wait so long for his breakfast!

Poor Oona was running out of places to hide her eggs. Then Willow the cat, who was very clever, whispered in her ear.

"Are you sure?" clucked Oona.

"Pretty sure," purred Willow.

The next day the farmer could not find his breakfast egg *anywhere*.

He spent most of the day looking, then gave up in disgust and ate cereal instead.

The next day was the same. And the next. And the next. By the end of the week, the farmer had given up looking. Anyway, he was rather enjoying his cereal!

Three weeks later, a cheeping sound came from the henhouse, and all the animals gathered round to see Oona's six beautiful little chicks. Yes, Oona had laid her eggs in the one place the farmer didn't think of looking – back in the henhouse!

The proud mother marched round the farmyard with her brood, and even the farmer couldn't help smiling. He was even more pleased a few months later, when the chicks were grown up and he had more eggs for his breakfast than he could ever eat!

The Cabbage Cruncher

Mr. Jameson's vegetable garden was his pride and joy. He had neat rows of carrots and cabbages, runner beans and radishes, peas and parsnips. There was not a weed, or a slug, or a caterpillar to be seen.

One morning Mr. Jameson had a shock. One of his cabbage leaves had been nibbled! The next morning, a whole cabbage was pretty much munched up.

That evening, Mr. Jameson made himself some sandwiches and a flask of coffee and settled down in his garden shed to keep watch.

Just as the moon was rising, someone came hopping into the garden. A little brown rabbit skipped happily over to the cabbages and started to nibble. A second later, he found himself nose to nose with Mr. Jameson, who had slipped out of the shed in his socks surprisingly quietly.

"What do you think you're doing?" he snarled.

"I'm just a poor, hungry bunny," sobbed the rabbit, "trying to keep going in these hard times. Sob!"

"Good acting," said Mr. Jameson grimly, "but not convincing. You don't look very hungry." Indeed, the cabbage cruncher was pretty plump.

The rabbit looked shrewdly at Mr. Jameson and tried another approach. "I'm so sorry," he said humbly, "but these are just the most beautifully grown, tenderest, juiciest, most delicious cabbages I have ever tasted. I couldn't help myself."

"Hmmmmmph," said Mr. Jameson, but he couldn't help feeling pleased. "It's not really me you need to worry about," the rabbit went on. "It's my cousins. There are hundreds of them. When I tell them about these vegetables...."

Mr. Jameson looked at the rabbit, and the rabbit looked right back.

"If I grew some very, very special cabbages, just for you," said the gardener, "do you think you could keep away from these fairly ordinary ones? And do you think your cousins would need to hear about it?"

"If I was busy dining on your very, very special cabbages, I wouldn't ever have time to see them," smiled the rabbit.

Mr. Jameson and the rabbit live happily side by side these days. And the clever little rabbit is even plumper.

Carenza the Cockatoo

Carenza was a beautiful white cockatoo. She was not a vain bird, but people seemed to like her, so she was proud of her snowy feathers and curly crest. Everything changed when Prudence the parrot began to share her cage.

Prudence was red and blue and green. She looked wonderful. People crowded around the cage to admire her – far more than had admired Carenza.

Carenza began to feel sad. She looked down at her plain feathers and felt, well, under-dressed. Prudence didn't help.

"I do think it's important to have at least a few green feathers," she would say. "They help the red ones look even brighter."

Carenza lost confidence. Her crest flopped, and she lurked at the back of the cage. No one wanted her any more.

Then, one day, the little girl who looked after the birds left the cage door open by mistake. Prudence shuddered and turned away. She was not an adventurous bird. But Carenza had seen something out in the room. Boldly, she stepped outside the cage door and flew over to the table.

The little girl had left her paints there. Carenza knew just what to do. Within a couple of minutes she had given herself a blue head, a red tummy, one purple wing, one pink wing, a yellow crest and a green back. The colours ran into each other a little bit, but she still thought she looked pretty good.

Just then the little girl returned. Carenza flapped her wings proudly and took up a pose. The little girl didn't smile or clap her hands in admiration. She screamed.

People came running from every direction.

"Oh, my goodness, is it a disease?" cried the little girl's mother. "I've never in my life seen such an awful looking bird."

"But she was so beautiful!" sobbed the little girl.

A visiting uncle, who understood at once what had happened, gently picked Carenza up and took her away to clean her.

Carenza didn't mind a bit. When she returned, her crest was standing up proudly as she joined Prudence in the cage. The admiring look in the little girl's eyes told her everything she needed to know, and she was happy to be herself once more.

Wiggly Worms

Josh loved to help his dad in the garden. Well, Josh called it helping. Sometimes his dad called it other things. Josh was only a little boy, so he couldn't dig or push the wheelbarrow. What he liked to do best of all was to clomp along in his red rubber boots on the soil that his dad had just dug.

One day, as Josh was clomping, he saw something very interesting. It was pink and wriggly. He bent down to pick it up.

"What's this, Dad?" he called.

Dad took one look and shouted, "It's a worm, Josh. Put it down carefully. Don't squish it. Don't squash it. And whatever you do, don't try to eat it!"

Josh didn't want to eat the worm, but he didn't want to put it down, either. He put it in his pocket instead.

That afternoon, Josh had a lovely time. He found eight more worms. Eight times his dad told him to put them down. But he didn't.

At four o'clock, Josh went indoors. He hung up his coat in the hall. He didn't think about the worms, but later, he had spaghetti for his supper, and looking down at his plate reminded him of the squiggly things in his pocket.

"I've just got to go and do something," he told his dad, wriggling down from the table.

"Josh, I told you to go before you sat down," said his mother, but Josh had already left the room.

He hurried to the hall and put his hand into his coat pocket. It was empty. He tried the other pocket. That one was empty, too. Josh looked on the floor, but there was no sign of anything squiggly or wiggly. He went back to his spaghetti with a thoughtful look on his face and somehow didn't feel like eating it after all.

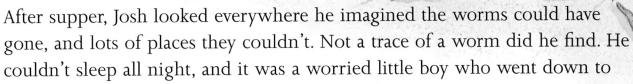

After supper, Josh looked everywhere he imagined the worms could have gone, and lots of places they couldn't. Not a trace of a worm did he find. He couldn't sleep all night, and it was a worried little boy who went down to

breakfast that morning. His mother asked him if he was feeling all right.

Dad was in a hurry as usual. Waving a piece of toast, he said goodbye to his family and hurried off to put on his coat and catch his train.

Josh was just beginning to think that he was so worried he really *did* feel ill, when there came a terrible yell from the hall.

Josh's mother rushed off to see what had happened, but Josh started spooning in the cereal he had pushed away. He had a big grin on his face and suddenly felt very, very hungry.

A Bird's-eye View

Once upon a time there were three friends who went for a walk in the woods. They were Kitty Cat, Roly Dog and Bobby Rabbit.

"Where are you off to?" asked Biddy Bird. "Can I come?"

"Don't be silly," said Kitty. "We're going for a walk. Birds like you don't walk. You fly. Of course you can't come."

Biddy Bird was upset. "I *can* walk," she said. "Look!"

But Biddy Bird could only hop.
And she couldn't hop quickly like Bobby Rabbit.

"No, no, that's no good," said Roly Dog.
"We're going to walk quickly. See you later!"

So the friends set off. Biddy Bird sat on a branch and felt sad. She hated being left out.

Meanwhile, Kitty and Roly and Bobby walked quickly through the woods. Pretty soon they were very tired.

"I think we should go home now," said Roly. "Come on!"

But which way was home? There were so many paths!

"We're lost," said Bobby.

"Completely lost," agreed Kitty.

"If only we hadn't walked so fast, we might have noticed where we were going," sighed Roly.

Just then, they heard a whistling sound overhead.

"I can help you!" called Biddy Bird.
"From up here I can see where all the paths lead."

So Biddy Bird helped the friends to find their way home.
Perhaps you can help Biddy.

I don't think Roly and Kitty and Bobby will leave Biddy behind
another time, do you?

The Perfect Picnic

Max Mouse looked out of the window. It was a beautiful sunny day. "Can we have a picnic in the park today, Mamma?" he asked.

"If you leave me in peace this morning and I can get all my work done, we can," said his mother.

So Mamma sat at the table with her papers, and Max sat with her and did some scribbling of his own until…

"Stop!" said Mamma, "you're writing on my work, Max! Now I'll have to do it all again!"

Next, Mamma went into the kitchen and cleared up the breakfast things. Max helped until…

"Stop!" cried Mamma. "You're spilling milk on the floor! Now I'll have to wash that as well!"

When the kitchen was tidy, Mamma went upstairs to collect all the dirty laundry. Max helped to carry it until…

"Stop!" called Mamma. "Those are clean clothes! Now I'll have to sort them all out again."

Max was very hungry by the time Mamma looked at the clock and said, "Oh dear, we'll have to have a late lunch."

"A late picnic," Max reminded her.

"Oh, yes, well, come on, let's get it ready," said his mother.

So they put sandwiches and apples and drinks and yogurts in a bag. Mum answered two phone calls and Max lost one of his trainers, but at last they were ready to go, until…

"Oh no!" said Max. As he opened the front door, there was a loud clap of thunder and rain came pouring down.

Max and Mamma looked at each other. Then Mamma began to laugh. "It's just not our day, Max," she said, "but I've got an idea."

Five minutes later, Max and Mamma were sitting in the middle of the playroom having a wonderful picnic until … the phone began to ring.

"The phone, Mamma!" said Max, when she didn't move.

"I can't hear the phone all the way from the park, can I?" grinned Mamma, staying right where she was. "Let's have another sandwich."

The Sausage Dog

There was once a dog who loved sausages.
He looked a bit like a sausage himself,
and his name was Bruno.

One morning, Bruno was strolling down the street
when he smelled something very interesting. Sausages!
He dashed into Mrs. Potter's house with a glint in his eye. Ten seconds later,
he dashed out again with a string of sausages in his mouth!

"Come back!" yelled Mrs. Potter, dashing out herself.

But Bruno scurried off down the street. Mrs. Potter was quite old. When she
got to the end of the street, she was out of breath.

"I'll help you," said Jimmy Jacks, who was on his way to the park. And he
rushed off after Bruno and the sausages.

Jimmy was fast, but Bruno had a good start. By the time he and Mrs. Potter
reached the next corner, they were both out of breath.

"I'll help," panted Mr. Markham, who was out for his morning jog.

But by the time Mr. Markham and Jimmy Jacks and Mrs. Potter reached the park gates, Bruno and the sausages were even further ahead.

"Woof!" barked a voice nearby. It was Bruce, a dog who liked sausages almost as much as Bruno did. He meant, "I'll help!" in dog language.

So Bruce and Mr. Markham and Jimmy Jacks and Mrs. Potter raced across the park. And although Bruno was fast, his legs were much, much shorter than Bruce's. Bruno reached the edge of the lake with Bruce right behind him.

"Woof! Woof!" barked Bruce, meaning "Drop those sausages!"

"Woof!" barked Bruno, meaning "No way!" But when Bruno opened his mouth to bark, the sausages dropped out, and Bruce quickly grabbed them.

Bruce laid the sausages at panting Mrs. Potter's feet. Mrs. Potter hesitated. Did she really *want* sausages that had been in the mouths of two dogs and dragged halfway across town? She did not. "You can have them, Bruce," she said, "for being such a good dog."

Mrs. Potter, Jimmy Jacks and Mr. Markham walked home. Bruce and Bruno went behind a bush and divided the sausages between them.

"Woof!" said Bruce, with his mouth full.

"Woof! Woof!" agreed Bruno happily. "It works every time!"

Moon Muncher

Oscar was a very small owl. He lived with his parents in a huge oak tree. For the first few weeks of his life all he could think about was food. He opened his little beak and waited for his mother or father to pop something delicious into it. And they did, all night long.

When Oscar got a little bit older, he started to take an interest in other things, too. He found out about his tree and all the other creatures who lived there, although he did not often meet them. Most of them were asleep at night, but Oscar and his family preferred to sleep during the day.

Then, one night, Oscar noticed something else. It was big and round and shiny. It hung among the stars just over the branch where Oscar was sitting.

"It's the moon," explained the little owl's dad. "Isn't it beautiful? We can see it every night if there are no clouds in the way."

The next night, it was a little later when Oscar woke up. He looked above his branch, but there was no moon! "Dad! Dad!" called Oscar.

Dad laughed. "The moon moves across the sky each night," he said. "Look over there!"

It was the moon, looking as beautiful as ever. Oscar was happy.

But over the nights that followed, Oscar became more and more worried. He wasn't sure at first, but at last he knew he was right. Something was eating the moon! It wasn't big and round any more. It was only about half the size it used to be.

Oscar decided that he must find out who was doing this terrible thing. Night after night, he sat on his branch and didn't take his eyes off the slowly moving moon.

"I'm worried about our Oscar," said his mother. "He's hardly eating at all. He just stares at the moon all night."

"I'll have a word with him," promised Dad.

By this time, only a tiny sliver of moon was left. When Dad went to talk to Oscar, he found the little owl crying. "Look at the moon, Dad," sobbed Oscar. "Tomorrow it will all be gone. The moon-muncher has eaten it up."

Dad smiled. "But a new moon will grow, Oscar," he said. "You just wait and see."

Dad was right. Each night, the moon grew a little bit bigger until one night, it was big and round and perfect, and Oscar was happy again.

The Circus Mouse

Titchy Mouse's granny came to stay one winter. She brought Titchy a present. It was a storybook about a circus, and Titchy loved it.

"I'm going to be in a circus one day," he told his little brother Teensy. "I'm going to be a famous tightrope-walker."

Titchy knew that he had some studying to do. He looked out of the window of the old tree stump where his family lived. There was just the thing! His mother had strung her laundry line between two bushes. It was perfect for tightrope-walking.

Getting onto the rope was easy. Titchy climbed up the bush and scampered onto the swaying line. *Ooooo...errrrr!* The line twizzled. Titchy twizzled ... and fell *bump!* on his head.

Teensy laughed so much that tears dripped off his tiny, baby nose.

"Right," said Titchy, brushing himself down. "I might be better at trapeze work." He had often watched the squirrels leaping through the branches of the nearby trees. It didn't look too hard.

Titchy climbed the nearest tree and took a huge leap towards the next branch. He didn't even come close. With a wail he crashed down toward the ground. Luckily, twigs and leaves broke his fall. He landed with a *crunch!*

right next to Teensy, who laughed and laughed until his ears went bright pink.

Titchy sat on the ground and thought. Maybe he really wasn't cut out for an act that took place in the air. What could he do on the ground. "I know!" he cried. "I'll be a lion-tamer!"

In a nearby garden lived an orange cat called Leo. "He'll be fine to practise on until I can find a real lion," said Titchy.

So Titchy armed himself with a chair and set off to find Leo.

It was easy. The cat was asleep in the sun. He didn't like being prodded with a chair, even if it was a tiny one. He gave a yelp and ran off, with Titchy running after him.

"Come back!" yelled Titchy. "I want you to do some tricks!" But Leo just ran faster.

The sight of a mouse chasing a cat sent Teensy into even more giggling and chortling.

"I don't know what's got into you today," said his mother. "You're not usually as cheerful as this, Teensy."

Titchy was catching his breath when he heard this. Suddenly, he knew exactly what he could be. He found a red berry and stuck it on his nose. He found a pair of his dad's shoes and some baggy trousers. He was a clown! And his antics kept Teensy laughing all afternoon.

Titchy had found his dream job at last.

The Magician's Rabbit

Mr. Magic was a magician. He performed at children's parties mainly.

The highlight of Mr. Magic's act was when he pulled a rabbit out of a hat. The audience always clapped and cheered at that point, and that made Mr. Magic happy.

One day, as Mr. Magic got his things ready for a show, the rabbit, who was sitting in the special, comfortable box that Mr. Magic had made for him, suddenly spoke!

"I'm very sorry," said the rabbit with a sigh, "but we won't be able to do the show today. I'm feeling really poorly."

Mr. Magic stood there with his mouth open for a moment. Then he realized what the rabbit had said.

"Do you need a vet?" he asked. "Will you be okay?"

"I'll be fine," said the rabbit. "It's just a cold. But I really couldn't work today. You'll have to tell the children they can't have their show."

"Well," said Mr. Magic, "I'm sorry you're ill, of course. And I want to talk to you later about the fact that you can *speak*. But I'll just do the show by myself and finish with the old patterned handkerchiefs trick instead. It's not as good as you appearing, but it will do."

"You can't do that!" cried the rabbit.

"I can and I will!" replied Mr. Magic. And he shut the rabbit up in his box.

Oh dear. The show was a disaster. The disappearing drink didn't disappear. The magic knots wouldn't come undone. And the patterned handkerchiefs were white. All of them.

At the end of the show, there was no cheering. Mr. Magic was very upset.

"This has never happened before," he muttered, as he loaded his boxes back into his car.

"I told you," said a muffled voice.

It was the rabbit. Mr. Magic opened the box. "I told you not to do the show," said the rabbit, "but you wouldn't listen."

"You mean I was so upset that you were ill that I couldn't do anything right?" asked Mr. Magic.

"No, you noodle!" shouted the rabbit. "It isn't you who does the magic. It's me! Usually. I'm the magician."

Mr. Magic was stunned. "Prove it," he said.

"Remember I'm not well," groaned the rabbit. But still, he produced a cup of coffee out of thin air. Mr. Magic drank the coffee – he felt he needed it – and thought about what the rabbit had said. At last he spoke.

"I will rename my act "Mr. Magic and Co." he said. "No one will guess that you are really Mr. Magic and I am 'and Co.' Oh, and one more thing…."

"I know," said the new Mr. Magic. And he magicked the coffee cup away.

The Lady and the Bird

Many years ago, a very rich lady kept a beautiful bird in a cage.
The bird was not very big, but she was gorgeous. She had red and
pink and orange feathers. She hated living in a cage.

One day, the bird decided that enough was enough. "I want to go out and
about," she told the rich lady. "I want to be out in the open air. I want to see
everything and go everywhere."

"But if I let you out of your cage, you'll fly away," said the lady.

"No, I won't," said the bird. But, of
course, as soon as the lady opened the
door, she was off. She flew out through
the open window and into the street.

It was wonderful being outside, but
the bird knew nothing of city ways.
She had grown up in a rainforest far
away. She flew straight into a telephone
wire and hurt her wing.

The poor bird fluttered down onto a windowsill to rest. Almost at once, a huge cat pounced on her and hurt her other wing. The poor bird could hardly fly at all now. She hopped and fluttered from windowsill to windowsill. By evening, she was very hungry and very tired.

By luck, the bird had fluttered last of all onto her very own windowsill! She didn't realize it, but the lady, sitting sadly inside, spotted her and cried out with delight. She picked the bird up carefully and carried her to the cage.

But the little bird shuddered and hid her head under her wing. Even though she was tired and hurt and hungry, she liked being free.

The lady was not unkind, and she noticed. She put the bird down on a chair and went to get her some food and water.

When she came back, the lady was smiling and dressed to go out. As the little bird ate and drank, she explained her plan.

"I know you want to see the wide world," she said, "and so do I. Why don't we do it together? Hop onto my hat, and we can travel wherever we like."

The little bird looked up. The lady was wearing a beautiful red and pink and orange hat. In the middle there was a place where a red and pink and orange bird could sit very comfortably and never be noticed at all.

So that is what they did. If you ever see a lady in a large red and pink and orange hat, look carefully. She may not be alone!

Index of Themes